Sons and Gunslicks

Where was Emily Greathcart? The pretty young lady from Denver who had gone to Arizona to meet her dead fiancé's mother had vanished. Only a bloodstained jacket was found in an abandoned spring buggy hired from the Pike's Crossing livery stable.

Emily was the daughter of Big Jack Greatheart, ex-marshal and one-time tamer of brawling boom-towns. But Big Jack lay in his bed in Colorado, frustratingly crippled by arthritis and a shadow of his former self. So he called on unconventional detective Joshua Dillard. Joshua followed a cold trail and hot impulses into battle against ambitious cattleman Bart Waller and his gun-handy, womanizing son, Vincent.

No wonder he was soon up to his reckless neck in two-fisted, lead-slinging trouble!

Sons and Gunslicks

CHAP O'KEEFE

A Black Horse Western

ROBERT HALE · LONDON

ISBN 978-0-7090-8068-8

Robert Hale Limited
Clerkenwell House
Clerkenwell Green
London EC1R 0HT

Typeset by
Derek Doyle & Associates, Shaw Heath
Printed and bound in Great Britain by
Antony Rowe Limited, Wiltshire

1

A YOUNG MAN'S MISTAKES

Joshua Dillard, earlier an operative with the famous Allan Pinkerton Detective Agency of Chicago and New York, was often led on false and bloody trails during his career as a freelance troubleshooter.

This was neither to his discredit nor extraordinary. The justice-seekers of his time and place, which was the whole of the American western frontier, survived in a wild and violent land. Strong and competent – as they had to be – they also made mistakes. They hurt the people they cared for or served; they sometimes succumbed to tarnishing impulses.

Many had no notion of how to earn a fortune, let alone keep it.

Most of these features were exemplified in Joshua's handling of the Emily Greatheart affair, a commission which took him to Arizona in search of a dying man's missing daughter. Yet the major errors in the matter perhaps arose out of the flaws in another man's character – a young fellow who was dead before the case was put in Joshua's hands.

Frank Clamorgan was the son of John and Augusta. John Clamorgan, deceased several years, had been smart and hard-working, growing his Slash C ranch based on an old Mexican holding to thousands of rich acres of good grass amply supplied with permanent water. Eventually the Slash C, by absorbing neighbouring properties, formed a sprawling piece of excellent cattle country – the lion's share of the immense Welcome Valley.

After his death, his widow, Augusta, worked the holdings in name though responsibility for the physical operation had fallen to the Slash C range boss, Ramon Rubriz. John's son Frank wanted none of it – except the privileges and easy wealth.

'I ain't no cow-nurse,' he told his mother, a scowl marring his smooth young face.

'No, dear, and I never wanted the monotonous routine of ranch life to be yours either. We have Ramon Rubriz and the rest of the hired *vaqueros* for that.'

Mrs Clamorgan held a misguided excess of maternal fondness for her only child. She overlooked his naturally indolent disposition. At the age of twenty, he'd never earned a nickel that could rightly be called his own – made money – but he'd spent plenty on lording it in the Pike's Crossing saloons and on various short-lived hobbies.

It was inevitable that Frank's fleeting fancy should

alight on the old mine situated on the northern boundary of the family lands. Here the ragged foothills to the snow-dusted, indigo peaks of a far mountain range made a natural boundary and were the only real scar on the Slash C perfection. The irregular badlands took in ravines and arroyos choked with head-high brush. Prickly pear with vicious spines had taken over the dry, rocky slopes, making them tricky to negotiate. On the sloping wall of one of the gullies was the entrance to the mine.

The workings were said to be Spanish in origin, nigh on two centuries old, and had been walled up with rocks for as long as anyone could remember, maybe to keep out straying stock or to deter varmints seeking homes. The only watch kept on the waste-land was by the red-tailed hawks that circled inter-mittently in the thermals overhead. And the *gavilán's* interest was not in ore but nesting rodents.

Frank rowelled an unwilling roan mare up the disused branch trail. She shook her head, snorted and showed big yellow teeth that jingled the bit-pieces. 'Keep going, you ornery beast!' Frank said. 'I don't believe a hoss can be spooked by windies.'

The tall tales of Welcome Valley old-timers had it the old mine was 'ha'nted'.

The treacherous ascent over the loose surface safely accomplished, Frank slipped from his silver-mounted saddle and approached the wall of rock barring obvious entry to the mine's dark recesses.

The punishing sun was dropping but still hung like a great ball of fire in a gold and crimson sky. What attention he had on his footing was taken up by a consideration for rattlesnakes, known to lurk in the shadows of the crags. When he stumbled on a raised outcrop, he cursed mildly, kicked at it a second time pettishly.

It was then he noticed the offending rock was an exposed vein of dark quartz, protruding several inches above the general surface and about six inches wide. It angled off in the direction of the mine entrance, disappearing beneath prickly pear and weathered detritus.

Frank was no prospector and his knowledge of geology and minerals was trifling, but because he wanted to find something important, he made his find a bigger deal than it was. He kicked loose some more of the weathered stuff, gracing the pieces in his head with the title of specimens. And sure, they were somewhat out of the ordinary – heavy in his hand and grey-blue on the outside. He smashed one against the rock wall. The late sun bounced back sparkles of light from its exposed core.

Silver! Frank thought, and next day took his samples to an assayer in Pike's Crossing.

The man was unimpressed, but he knew he was dealing with the heir to the richest spread in Welcome Valley, and folks had long gotten out of the habit of upsetting Clamorgans. He clapped an eyeglass to it, his squint disguising his true assessment.

'It's galena, the most important ore and the principal source of lead,' he mumbled to Frank. 'It's made up of lead sulphide, but chance is there's considerable silver associated. Hundred ounces to the ton if'n you're lucky. Could be other accessory metals likewise – mebbe a little gold. . . .'

The word was enough for Frank. Courtesy of his doting mother, who untied the purse strings with her usual alacrity, he was promptly riding a ticket to Denver, Colorado. At this time, more mining machinery was built in the mile-high city than in any other centre in the world. Frank was going to order all he needed to restart the mine.

Leastways, that was his intention before he stepped into one of the substantial, brick-built shops in Larimer Street to buy a box of his favourite cigars. There he met and was figuratively bowled over by Miss Emily Greatheart who was working behind the store's counter.

She wore a dark green, neat business suit with a tightly cut bodice which revealed a shapely figure as perfect as her delicately formed ivory-skinned face and high-piled red-gold hair. Frank was flattered by her attentive manner and instantly decided she was the epitome of city sophistication – elegant, cultured, refined. Yet she was somehow small and fragile-looking at the same time. Excitement coursed in Frank, because he sensed this girl of such great charm and beauty was as much impressed by him as he by her.

Though his mouth went dry he managed, before completing his purchase and leaving, to make an invitation. 'I'm so rushed,' he said. 'Would you mind wrapping my cigars in brown paper and bringing them to my hotel around supper time?'

'Of course, sir. It will be a pleasure.'

'Perhaps you'd like to share my table, to dine with me?'

'Why, that would be lovely!' the vision breathed. 'Thank you.'

Both were naïve in many respects. Though Frank didn't realize it, his rapid decision that Emily Greatheart had sophistication was based on his illusions – a relative judgement based on knowledge limited to girls in and around Pike's Crossing, a backwater. His initial good impression arose from the tutored responses of a helpful shop assistant; hers from response to a face tanned by Arizona sun and to an easy drawl.

But Emily's natural, youthful charm did extend beyond the bounds of a counter. One meeting led to another and before a week was out, Frank was totally captivated. Emily lived with a widower father whose health was not robust, and they were unchaperoned, unadvised. The Arizonan wooed her in a lightning romance and they became engaged to be married.

Frank Clamorgan returned to his home in the Southwest alone but cock-a-hoop. His beautiful wife-to-be would follow as soon as she could resign her position at the Larimer Street store and housekeeping arrangements were finalized for her pa.

Augusta Clamorgan received her eager son's glad news as though she didn't know whether to laugh or cry.

'Oh, Frank!'

'Why've you gotten tears in your eyes, Mom? She's a grand filly.'

'They're not tears. It's just that—'

He went to her and she put her arms around him.

'Emily's real pretty,' he said. 'It'll work out fine.'

She stiffened, taking a grip. 'Son, you're committing yourself to something. How do you know this shop gal is worthy? You're too young to know what you're letting yourself in for.'

'Why do you have to make things difficult?' he burst out petulantly.

But she didn't, wouldn't reply and Frank, thoroughly disgruntled, took himself to the stable where he saddled up his roan mare to take himself into town. At bottom, pursuit of pleasure was the sum total of his aspirations in life and he didn't like having his actions criticized by his doting mother. He wasn't used to that *a-tall*.

Where could he turn? What could he do?

Like many a man in a moment of weakness, he turned to liquor. He shouldered in through the batwings of the Golden Horse saloon in Pike's Crossing, sauntered to the counter and caught the apron's eye. He slapped his wallet on the slop-stained mahogany and reached out to stop the bottle and glass that came sliding down to him from the attentive barkeeper. It made a fellow feel good to command respect and immediate attention to his wants, he thought.

He filled the glass, emptied it in a couple of gulps and refilled it. Before long he was feeling a mite giddy, a little drunk. . . . Naw, he wasn't drunk! Just mellow. It was all one with the bright lamps, the tobacco smoke and the tinny piano music in the background.

He thumbed through his wallet and found his

picture of Emily. She was damn pretty, that was for sure. And he was going to put a ring on her finger, make every delicious inch of her in the flesh all his. He poured more of the strong liquor to celebrate the coming thrill of it.

'I'd go easy on that stuff,' a voice said at his elbow. 'Might make yuh too limp for Mattie's gals.'

The speaker was Jake Phelps, a Rocking W hand; built like a king rat, small head, big body. Mattie ran the local whorehouse.

'Don't need no soiled doves!' Frank snapped at his provoker. 'I'm saving myself for a girl I met in Denver. She's coming to marry me.'

Vincent Waller himself, son of the second biggest rancher in Welcome Valley and Phelps's employer, joined in the taunting.

'Some raddled lady of the night you met walking Market Street, huh?'

'No, Waller, you dumb ox! Look – this is her picture. See for yourself how beautiful she is.'

The hand who'd started it said artfully, 'Why, sure, she's a smooth hide. An' when she turns up, guess she'll soon notice han'some Vince here.' He drew closer to Frank, nudged him, winked and rasped into his ear, 'It's s'posed to be private but Vince sparks all the pretty she-noodles in this neck o' the woods. Has 'em hoistin' their skirts an' slippin' their drawers to someplace round their parted knees sweet an' quick as drippin' honey. Must be somethin' to do with his fam'ly bein' up-an'-comin' an' all.'

The barb was designed to strike in several directions. Vince had a voracious desire for women which was alleged in confidence to be accommodated with or, on occasion, without co-operation. Meanwhile, the rapid growth of the Rocking W was driven by the ego and paranoia of the young stud's father, Bart Waller, who was determined to wrest power in the country from the long-established Clamorgan interests.

'Emily ain't like that,' Frank said hotly, seeing no further than his current interest and the insulting challenge to his brag. 'You got no right to talk like Emily's a – a whore! Her pa is Big Jack Greatheart, an ol' time lawman and gunfighter who cleaned up boom towns.'

'Yeah, you got no right, Jake Phelps – shuddup!' Vince said. 'Do tell, Frank – what boom towns were these?'

Frank screwed up his face the better to produce an answer from his drink-fuddled memory. 'Abilene. . . .'

'Oh?' Vince said. 'Thought that was some other jasper.'

'Well, mebbe it was Dodge. . . .'

'Mebbe so. Or Ellsworth or Wichita,' Vince added, smirking. 'Come to think, way you're talking, this old man could be Wyatt Earp hisself!'

Whereupon, with gales of laughter, the Waller bunch departed for an upstairs room to play five-card stud.

Frank had hoped his talk of a gunfighting lawman might have impressed them – after all, most of 'em were gunslicks themselves, hired by Bart Waller more for their gun-handy, bully-boy ways than their range skills. It was only later, and after Frank had downed still more bonded whiskey, that he noticed his chaste picture of Emily was missing from the counter.

He groped through the thick wad of greenbacks in his wallet and it wasn't there either. Nor in his pants pockets. It must have been that funning Vince Waller and his rannies; they'd gone too far and filched it while his gaze was diverted!

He shook his head to clear the cobwebs and lurched toward the staircase to the upper floor, determined to retrieve his stolen treasure.

At the foot of the stairs, an advertisement was fixed to the wall. His weaving path brought it into focus when he was really close. Under a painting of a voluptuous nude, discriminating gentlemen's attentions were respectfully drawn to the pleasures to be had at Mattie's Boarding House on a nearby cross street. The names and photographs of several girls were appended – Sadie and Irene and Queenie . . . and Emily!

Someone had tacked Frank's picture to the advertisement after scrawling on it in heavy pencil '*Emily – Cuming Attrackshun*'.

This time the insult to Emily – or maybe it was to his pride – hit home so Frank couldn't ignore it despite the mellowness.

'The goddamned bastards!' he blurted, his face darkening. He tore down the picture and pounded up the stairs.

A well-placed kick slammed open the door to the card-players' smoky sanctum.

Vince Waller dropped his hand and jumped from

his chair. On the baize-covered table chips were scattered and drinks slopped over.

'Chris'sakes, Clamorgan! You can't come busting in here!'

Frank roared, 'A man's entitled to defend his lady's honour, you dirty skunks!'

'Simmer down, kid,' Phelps warned. 'Yuh're drunk, an' yuh got a hell of a temper!'

Vince said, 'Aw, throw the asshole out, boys!'

The card game broke up in a hurry.

Frank lost his head and unholstered his forty-five. 'No one lays a hand on me. Stay put, the lot of you! I want the man that defiled Miss Greatheart's picture. He's gonna pay!'

'Pay what 'xactly?' Phelps said with deceptive mildness but distracting emphasis.

As Frank's gaze shifted, Vince threw himself to one side and grabbed for his own sidearm, cocking the hammer and squeezing the trigger all in the one eye-cheating movement.

Vince's revolver blasted. The shot screamed across the room, passed close to Frank's head and went out the door. Frank ducked involuntarily, feeling the scorching heat of the bullet as it sped past his face. He was almost blinded by the shocking, sobering nearness of death. When he jerked off a return shot, it went hugely wild.

Vince promptly fired again.

Frank staggered from the impact of the slug, which felt like a mighty blow to his chest. Mortally hit, he fell back, exclaiming, 'I'm shot!' His gun fell with a thud from a suddenly limp and nerveless hand, and then he was on the floor, unable to talk, with a roaring in his ears and hot blood oozing through his cold fingers.

It was over in seconds.

'Get Doc McAdams!' someone said.

'Too late fer that, the poor damned idiot,' Phelps said. 'That was the saltiest, dumbest play I ever saw.'

Drawn by the gunfire, a curious crowd gathered cautiously in the saloon below. The boldest started to edge up the stairs to investigate, the apron to the fore.

The news was passed down. 'Frank Clamorgan's been killed!'

Vince's impassive, even-featured face betrayed nothing.

'He got a shuck in his snoot and asked for it. I reckon everyone saw what happened. Another Clamorgan gone. Reckon my old man will be pleased.'

'Sure. Thar's allus bin bad blood 'tween the families,' Phelps said. 'But if'n this Denver filly gits to show up, *she* ain't gonna be pleased, Vince. I hope y'all c'n – uh – comfort Miss Emily Greatheart.'

Vince stooped and retrieved the picture from where it had fluttered down and was now alongside Frank's bleeding corpse.

He examined it speculatively. 'Reckon I could give it a damned good try, Phelps. Why, it'd be a *pleasure*.'

2

WHERE IS EMILY?

Big Jack Greatheart directed Joshua Dillard to the straightbacked chair at his bedside with a weak wave of a wasted, twisted hand.

Joshua was appalled. The famous ex-marshal he'd come to see in his handsome, two-storey brick house in Denver was no more than a living skeleton, a mere shadow of his former self. Many had once admired him; badmen had feared him in the heady days when he'd tamed more than one lawless town on the western frontier. Now his once tall and powerful frame was reduced to skin and bone. The gaunt face amid the pillows propping him up was of a papery, yellow-ish complexion in the lamplight.

'Set, Mr Dillard,' he said in a voice that had lost the means to boom. 'It was good of you to come.'

'I come out of considerable respect, sir, as well as the obligation to earn a living,' Joshua said.

'Ah, yes,' Big Jack said. 'Your financial position

hasn't been good since you – uh – retired from the Pinkertons, I hear.'

Joshua replied with customary frankness. 'No, it ain't. I come to the bottom of the barrel mighty often these days, but I'm ready to go half-shod when a job takes my fancy. I hate cheaters and lawbreakers.'

'They say you're very good with a gun,' Big Jack said questioningly.

'If it's called for, I'll comb the right heads with a six-shooter even when the client's dinero don't add up to the squarest deal.'

Big Jack nodded approvingly. 'You're just the man needed; after my own heart, you might say. These days I don't get the chance to pull irons out of fires no more. The arthritis, y'understand.'

Joshua ran over what he knew about Greatheart in his mind.

Big Jack had wisely withdrawn from his peace-officer career in early midlife and secured himself a position as a journalist in Denver with the *Rocky Mountain News*, the influential paper founded by the astute William N. Byers in 1859. Unfortunately, as the years had passed, and just as he'd carved himself a successful new niche, his health began to fail.

A crippling illness for which the Denver doctors could find no cure chopped away at his powerful physique. He grew crusty and bed-ridden; lost his wife in an outbreak of influenza; apparently became in large measure dependent on his uncomplaining daughter, Emily, who was his only child.

'I'm financially comfortable, Mr Dillard,' Big Jack said forthrightly. 'I've got a bit of money stashed away

– enough to make the employment worth your while, regardless of other considerations.'

He filled a briar pipe with fumbling fingers. Joshua found it almost painful to watch him pull the tobacco from a buckskin pouch and pack it in, but knew it would further demean the broken man to offer to help.

'Obliged to hear the details of your problem, in your own time, of course,' Joshua said.

After requesting Joshua's assistance in the striking of a match, Big Jack got his pipe drawing to his satisfaction, cleared his throat and began to talk of his beautiful girl, Emily. She was the light of his life and the attractive young woman whose picture was on his bedside table.

Though the subject's formal posture for the photograph made her look stiff, even severe, Joshua put that down to the dictates of the portrait taker, for her smile was open and warm. It was a face both charming and very alive, which made the suggestion of her death in Big Jack's tale all the more distressing.

'Emily has disappeared in Arizona,' he said, 'but I get ahead of myself and must begin at the beginning. . . .'

Big Jack explained how his daughter had met and quickly – possibly rashly – become engaged to Frank Clamorgan, son of a prominent rancher in Welcome Valley, almost six months back.

'You know how it is with a lightning courtship,' he said apologetically. 'Some times young folks can't think straight on account of their strong passions.'

It had not been possible for Emily to travel with the excited lad when he went back to Arizona, since she'd had to give proper notice to her employer in Larimer Street and arrange for a housekeeper and nurse to take over the management of her pa's care and their home.

Big Jack sighed. 'She was in love and happy, but it was all blighted when news came that the boy had gotten himself shot in a card room over a saloon.'

Emily couldn't rush immediately to Arizona, as she was inclined, and accepted her pa's wise counsel on the futility in such a move. The weeks went by and Emily felt more and more beholden to go pay her respects at her fiancé's last resting place and to his distressed mother.

The Greathearts had corresponded with a Doctor Denholm McAdams, the physician in Pike's Crossing, who said he'd been the closest friend of Frank's father, old John Clamorgan, and was now his widow, Augusta Clamorgan's medical adviser and confidant.

Doctor McAdams said Mrs Clamorgan, who was sinking in a morass of grief, might find a visit by Emily comforting and calming.

Accordingly, the arrangements were put in place. A Mrs Martha Fardell, a follower of the teachings of the Sisters of Charity of Leavenworth who'd founded Denver's St Vincent's Hospital, was put in charge of Big Jack's household. Free of filial duty, Emily made the long journey south by railroad through Colorado into New Mexico, then west by stagecoach to Arizona. She had a room reserved at the hotel in the township of Pike's Crossing. From this base, she could go visiting with her fiancé's mother at the *hacienda* on the Clamorgan cattle spread, using a rented buggy.

Big Jack's voice was laden with despair.

'Emily arrived safely at the Slash C, was seen to leave, but never made it back to Pike's Crossing. A docile, well-behaved horse brought the spring buggy back to the livery stable empty. The only sign Emily had ever been in the thing was the quilted jacket she wore.'

Big Jack added brokenly, 'They say that it was found on the seat – bloodstained.'

'Helluva thing,' Joshua growled. 'You've been in touch with the sheriff's office in Pike's Crossing?'

'Sure. I was telegraphed 'bout it. They were mystified as anybody, they claimed.' He scowled and spots of colour appeared on his sallow cheeks. 'The blasted fools asked if my gal was a young woman of – uh – good reputation. Like to say she might-a strayed off someplace with somebody for unwholesome purposes.'

Joshua tutted. 'Ignorant . . . tactless. Didn't they scour the countryside for her?'

'A Sheriff Horace Sherman fossicked around some, sent out trackers, found nary a damn' thing. Nor did a search of her hotel room yield anything in the way of clues. I tell you, the job needs a proper range detective. I've no faith in these hick, johnny-come-lately law enforcers. They quit too fast.'

Joshua nodded. 'Yeah. Hard work and dedication have gotten in short supply among the tin-star toters.'

With a trace of the fire and the dominant spirit that had forged his reputation, Big Jack snapped, 'Weren't like it in my day!'

Joshua committed himself instantly. He'd been going up against appointed and elected marshals, sheriffs and constables for years. Even as a Pinkerton agent he'd been obliged to toe certain legal and political lines. Since, he'd enjoyed the freedom he'd had as a freelance, self-employed troubleshooter, responsible in the final analysis to no one but himself. He knew also, from personal experience, the pain of losing a loved one.

His wife! Killed all those years ago now in San Antone. Gone, gone . . . yet always with him, possessing him, motivating him. Turning him into an emotional cripple, too. Undermining his good sense. The Wilder gang's murder of his woman, chiefly because he was a Pinkerton, had led to his resignation from the agency and his obsession with hunting lawbreakers. Bringing them to book. *Killing* them.

Some said bluntly that Dillard was a professional gunman, a bounty man, a killer for hire. At times he'd been all of these things, though clinging to a personal code of ethics peculiarly his own and shaped by his grim experience. This code was at once the source of his strength and the seed of his failures, which were largely monetary.

Maybe because of his unbusinesslike approach, Joshua lost financially on most of his assignments, picking up no more than expenses. His bank balance was constantly dwindling. Realistically, cases that were within the law and that he might choose to handle were few and far between. Moreover, he couldn't be bothered with any unless the fee was right, given what the client could afford to pay, and unless the job appealed.

Finding Big Jack's daughter did appeal. What looked like foul play involving a pretty young woman struck close to his heart. He didn't doubt his late intervention on a trail evidently allowed to grow cold would be difficult.

Too, his interest would be resented by the local peace officers. They'd be jealous of his reputation and his ability to probe without consideration of the community's sensitivities. But no nevermind. He'd do it to help a good man who was down and hurting from his impotence in the matter.

Thus it was that Joshua agreed to pick up the abandoned scarch for the missing Emily Greatheart, seeing it as worthy of his time and energy, though not especially profitable to his purse.

'I'm very grateful to you, Mr Dillard,' Big Jack said. 'Now if you don't mind, maybe you'd run along. That might sound churlish, I guess, but I tire very easily from the fretting. Knowing you're on the job takes some of the load off my mind . . . might at last allow me some sleep.'

Before Joshua was out the door, Big Jack's chin had dropped forward on to his sunken chest.

Joshua arrived in Pike's Crossing on the afternoon stage. He was the sole passenger, and the whip's attention was immediately given to unloading express from the coach's railed top.

Disembarking, dropping his slack, half-filled warbag at his feet and easing the kinks out of his long limbs, Joshua cast his faded blue eyes over his new surroundings. He noted how the stage stop was conveniently situated in front of the only hotel, the unaptly named two-storey Grand, and how similar the township was to a hundred other two-bit ranching burgs he'd passed through in his nomadic life.

A wide and dusty main street separated two ranks of false-fronted stores and business houses. A couple of dogs napping in the shade under the plankwalks opened curious eyes, but settled down again. A bewhiskered oldster spat a stream of brown tobacco juice into the roadway from the creaking chair he occupied on the Golden Horse saloon's porch.

It was in that establishment, behind one of the opaque-looking upstairs windows, that Frank Clamorgan had rashly drawn his gun and met a violent and early death.

Beyond the commercial section were a cluster of residences and a whitewashed church in one direction and a scatter of Mexican *jacals* bounded by the east bank of the river and the bridge in the other.

'Mr Dillard?'

The man who approached him, breaking off his appraisal, was a short and stocky gent, probably crowding sixty, but near-white hair and a bushy grey beard cut spade fashion might have made him look older than his years.

'I'm Dillard.'

For travel in the unglazed, leather-curtained Concord coach, Joshua wore a long duster draped

24

from square-set shoulders over coat and pants shiny with wear. Crumples were evident in the broad brim of his flat-crowned black hat.

'And you must be Doctor McAdams,' he guessed.

He needn't have worried about his worn garb giving a first impression of shabbiness. For the medico himself was not a picture of proud success. He was dressed in the black twill, three-piece suit of a professional man, but it was stained and unpressed. Even outdoors, a chemical fustiness clung to him. He looked the archetypal ageing bachelor.

'Indeed,' the doctor said. 'Mr Greatheart wrote me. Pleasure to meet you, though I fear your trip will be a wasted one.'

Joshua gripped and shook his large white hand. 'We'll have to see. I don't aim to come all the way down to Arizona to do nothing.'

'Well, no . . . but frankly, I'm inclined to believe Mr Greatheart's hopes are unrealistic and that it's best for his own health that he should come to terms with his loss.'

'We'll see,' Joshua repeated. Mentally, he checked off McAdams's disposition as saturnine.

It was arranged he should confer later with McAdams in his consulting rooms, after he'd taken up the booking made for him at the Grand Hotel.

The doctor's house and surgery were on a corner in the residential quarter. White paint on the picket fence was blistered and peeling. Tough weeds were the lot's dominant growth. Joshua opened the gate and took the walk to a small porch and side door, where a shingle said '*Office*' above the legend

'*Denholm McAdams, M.D.*' and, in smaller script underneath that, '*Homage to the Lord*'.

'Don't bother with the bell,' McAdams's voice called. 'Just come on in.' His tone was polite but seemed to suggest the interview was going to be an unnecessary chore, to be run through quickly.

Joshua went through a narrow hall.

McAdams sat behind a large desk in a room where a fire smouldered needlessly behind a brass fender. A lamp with an amber glass shade hung low over the desk, casting yet more glow.

'Pull up a chair and sit down, Dillard.'

Joshua did. Seated, the atmosphere in the darkly panelled room was even more claustrophobic. Indoors, McAdams's distinctive smell came close to overpowering. Of just what was it compounded?

'There's nothing you – we – can do for Mr Greatheart, you know that, of course—'

'Know nothing of the kind yet,' Joshua said, putting briskness into the contention. Distractedly, he placed the possible main component of McAdams's smell – gardenia toilet water. Overlaid some with carbolic. He dragged himself back to the subject in hand.

'Miss Emily Greatheart is a missing person. I'll look for her.'

McAdams shook his head gloomily. 'If you insist, and I guess you have to do something to earn your commission . . . but it has to be realized that only by the barest of chances could the young woman still be alive. What tidings do you want to carry to a father who by all accounts is close to – ah – passing over himself? Surely it's more merciful for the situation to stay unresolved, as it is.'

'If she's dead, why haven't her remains been found?'

'Best efforts failed,' McAdams said, spreading his hands. 'The trail to the Slash C and every inch of the bordering terrain were scoured by skilled trackers – men fit to follow a spider across a swept floor. How can you turn up anything now?'

Joshua reflected bitterly that on the face of it, and without a scrap of evidence to work on, the doctor's pessimism was well founded.

It looked like becoming one of the most daunting, frustrating assignments he'd tackled.

3

WARNINGS AND A FIGHT

The facts were grim, depressing and unhelpful: Emily had hired the spring buggy from the livery stable, taken the easy road out to the Slash C, visited with Mrs Augusta Clamorgan, placed the flowers she'd brought on her fiancé's sarcophagus in a private chapel, then departed. Yet she'd never arrived back in Pike's Crossing. Only the buggy came, drawn by the well-behaved horse returning to its stable. On the buggy seat was the bloodstained coat, but no other evidence of violent struggle.

Trackers said the sign on the trail showed the buggy had travelled unhurriedly, sedately, making several pauses.

'I'll go out to the Slash C myself,' Joshua said. 'I need to speak to the people who last saw Miss Greatheart. Can this be arranged?'

McAdams frowned. 'Mrs Clamorgan is a widow and a sick woman still stricken by the grief occasioned by the loss of her only son. The ranch business is conducted by the late Mr Clamorgan senior's top hand, Ramon Rubriz. On my advice, Augusta now no longer accepts visitors.'

Joshua fixed him with an intimidating stare. 'Is that so? What about your ownself? Don't she receive her doc?'

'Of course! Why, I'll be making a routine call at the Slash C tomorrow.'

'Then I'll ride along.'

McAdams pondered. 'Maybe I can arrange it. . . .'

'Damn right you can,' Joshua declared. 'That's what being a medico means in my book. Fixing folks up so they function normal. You do it.'

'Now, see here—' McAdams began coldly.

Joshua waved him down. 'I'm through talking,' he said, rising to his feet.

McAdams responded dryly, 'So it would seem.'

'Have no illusions. You won't stand in my way, and you've given me no good reason why you should.'

More so than before, McAdams set his face in a wooden, impersonal expression, as though to deter all inquiry into confidential details.

'Mrs Clamorgan is my patient, so naturally I'm reticent to use my good offices for the purposes you suggest. It would be unprofessional, conflicting with my oath to God maybe. . . .'

'The hell with that!' Joshua said incredulously, postponing his decision to leave. 'I want to know what happened to Emily Greatheart. So does her father, who's ex-marshal Jack Greatheart. Your patient's privacy seems kinda trivial when it comes to determining what fate befell a healthy young woman. I'll go hire myself a mount for tomorrow.'

'I wouldn't were I you,' the doctor said in a controlled voice. 'It'd be more – ah – convenient to ride alongside me in my buggy.'

'Why so?' Joshua became flinty again. 'I'd prefer sitting a horse than riding in a buggy like a city dude.'

McAdams drew a deep breath. 'You need to see the whole picture, Dillard. The Welcome Valley country lives on the edge of undeclared range war. Strange riders are apt to run into loose flying lead on account of the Clamorgan-Waller feud.'

Joshua had done his homework and knew in broad terms the circumstances of young Frank Clamorgan's death while drawing a gun on a fellow of roughly his own age – Vincent, the son of Bart Waller.

'I hear these Wallers have a high-handed way of doing things, running roughshod over peaceable folks.'

'Indeed,' McAdams agreed. 'Waller is the second biggest rancher in the valley. With my friend John Clamorgan dead, and now John's son, he aims to be king. The rapid growth of his Rocking W holdings is matched only by his escalating ego and paranoia. He's obsessive where rival Clamorgan interests are concerned. He's dragged everybody into the fight between the families, saying they're either for him or against him.'

Joshua sat down again. 'And tell me, Doc – where

do you stand?'

McAdams shrugged. 'With the Clamorgans naturally, though I'm the district's only physician and do
my duty when called on. As the Good Book says,
"Blessed are the peacemakers: for they shall be called
the children of God".'

Joshua grunted. 'Never had much time for "Love
your enemies".'

'Judge not, Dillard. Frontier medical practice
presents its dilemmas. That said, Bart Waller has paid
me well in the past to take care of complications aris-
ing out of what might be termed his son's romantic
adventures, and I've not seen fit to deny his young
female victims relief before their bellies could
expose their shame.'

'Well, call me vindictive,' Joshua said disdainfully.
'If there's one breed of louse that disgusts me, it's the
kind that have their way with women and don't give
a damn how much they make 'em suffer. I'd act to
put nooses around the bastards' necks faster than if
they'd shot a man in the back, or rustled cattle or
thieved hosses.'

McAdams stroked his bearded chin, thinking on
Joshua's words.

'Come to think on it, wouldn't surprise me if
young Vince Waller knew something about what
happened to Emily Greatheart. A smart-aleck, always
funning, fooling with the girls. . . . Him or his
daddy's wild crew, firing their guns at lone travellers
without cause or care. . . .'

He tailed off. His eyes searched Joshua's face for
reaction.

31

'Them observations are the most interesting you've made so far, Doc,' Joshua said.

For his part, McAdams essayed a conciliatory grin.

'A mean bunch, Dillard. You know, Waller's men look more like gunslicks than ranch hands or range riders to me. They won't take kindly to a man with your rep poking about in what they see as their territory. I'd watch out, firebrand though they say you are.'

Joshua's voice was hard. 'I'll be waiting for 'em.'

But about that he was wrong.

Joshua Dillard went back to the Grand Hotel. Passing through the prosaic lobby, he nodded, friendly fashion, to the clerk behind the desk. The man, a sad oldster with a straggly longhorn moustache, swiftly averted his eyes and fussed over the register.

'Plenty of fascinating characters in that book, I reckon, but not much of a narrative to speak of,' Joshua joked.

The clerk didn't laugh. In what appeared plumb rudeness, he acted like Joshua didn't exist. Joshua shrugged imperceptibly and started up the stairway. It was all part of the penalty of being Dillard, a man with a growing reputation for being on a scene when trouble broke; for sometimes butting into affairs that were none of his business; for spoiling for a fight. Moreover, the frontier press was apt to exaggerate – in point of fact, reporters and editors occasionally turned his exploits into sensationalism in the cause of selling newspapers. So it was no wonder if he wasn't welcome.

Arriving in the shadowy passage outside his room, Joshua brought up stock-still. The door he'd left closed and locked was ajar.

He drew the trusty Peacemaker that rode low on his lean right hip. The weapon was a well-worn, black-gripped example of the 1873 model Colt six-gun folk were told by the rumour-mongers he took money to use. Then he thrust open the door, stepping to one side.

Nothing totally shocking happened. No one shot at him; no one swung a club. But he saw four men were in his room. They were waiting and watching the door, making the dowdy place look more cramped than it was.

'Pardon me to hell for asking,' Joshua said with a harshness that was in no way apologetic, 'but just what the blazes are you jaspers doing in my room?'

A large, craggy-faced individual in a black Stetson, tall and big with a heavy gold watch-chain across his strained vest and a revolver making a bulge under his broadcloth coat tails, said, 'I'm Bart Waller, mister, and what we're doing is coming to ask what *you're* doing in *our* Welcome Valley.'

'Not enjoying any welcome, that's for sure,' Joshua said.

The four were spread across the confined space of his room in a threatening half-circle. To Waller's left was a younger man, resembling him in looks, but slighter in bulk. Joshua figured this had to be the speaker's son, Vincent Waller, the man who'd gunned down Frank Clamorgan.

Waller nodded curtly at Joshua's Peacemaker. 'Put

that thing up. Mebbe you could put a slug in one of us with it, but we're four and the second, third and fourth shots would go through your own hide.'

He was right. He'd go down in a smash of gunfire. Joshua holstered his weapon and folded his arms. 'Now what?'

'You this hell-on-wheels Dillard?'

'I'm Joshua Dillard.'

'Well, we don't need range dicks in this country. We take care of our own problems. And we don't want no has-been tramps with gunfighter reps. We heard the whispers. . . .'

Vincent Waller chorused, 'Yeah, we heard the whispers, you bet. How no amount of killing is ever enough to appease hell-on-wheels Dillard.'

That was rich, Joshua thought. The other two members of Waller's party were obvious hardcases – gunslick types with cold, watchful eyes and mocking grins. He'd never seen a finer case of the pot calling the kettle black.

'Except your own has-been gunfighters, of course,' he said, addressing only Bart Waller. 'And a fool son who I understand didn't hesitate any when it came to cutting down another Valley family's son.'

The big man's face turned ruddy. His son swore. 'Jesus, let's pile on to the smart-lipped galoot, Dad!'

'Hold it, Vince. The poor devil don't know who he's tangling with, what he's getting his sticky beak into.'

Joshua glared right back at them. 'I'm getting into looking for Emily Greatheart, young Clamorgan's fiancée, and I don't scare off easy.'

'The Clamorgan kid was an idiot, Dillard,' Waller said. 'Pay no heed to the lies put about by his mother and her hirelings.'

'He was allus showin' out,' Vince said. 'I shot him 'cause I had to.' He turned to one of the gunnies. 'You saw it, Phelps – tell him!'

'Ne'mind!' Waller snapped. 'I'm just saying, Dillard, we don't need your meddling. Frank Clamorgan weren't worth more'n a heap of horse chips – a vain, spoiled braggart who got his comeuppance.'

Joshua treated him to a sneer. 'So what about Emily Greatheart – she get her needings, too?'

'We never saw his scantlin'!' Vince protested. 'I never laid a hand on her!'

Joshua smiled at his vehemence. 'Well then, my looking into her disappearance should be just fine and dandy for you, shouldn't it?'

His father said, 'See here, Dillard, I'll speak plain – Vince didn't touch the gal. Mebbe she didn't want to return to her tough ol' daddy in Denver. Mebbe she'd a hankering to kick over the traces. She coulda skedaddled anyplace south, west or east. You might be tough as a boot and twice as high, but if you got sense you'll light out of Pike's Crossing on the next stage.'

'Been told to quit many a time afore,' Joshua said, shrugging. 'Strange – many of those plain speakers have ended up resting their busy lips in penitentiaries or boom-town Boot Hills.'

Hearing his boss answered back, Jake Phelps came to life with a growl. 'Thar'll come a day, wise guy! No

35

man's lucky streak lasts fer ever.'

Joshua showed his contempt for the paid sidekick, mean and bulky though he was, by ignoring him. With taunting deliberation, and seeking to trap Vince into a damning admission, he said, 'I hear you often get to taste a girl hereabouts before she goes to join her lover, kid.'

With a smothered curse, Vince lost his rag. '*Shi*. . . ! You'll get to taste my knuckles, asshole!' Face hot as an uncovered firepit, he waded into Joshua, swinging meaty fists.

Joshua realized his scheme was backfiring from hell to breakfast. If this became a free-for-all, the numbers said he was going to be the loser.

He ducked under Vince's initial punches, backing off out the door.

'Fight, bastard!' Vince screamed, but Joshua continued to retreat down the passage to the landing, returning only the mildest defensive jabs and concentrating on ducks, weaves and fancy, back-pedalling footwork.

Old man Waller and his gunslicks were bellowing like enraged bulls as they spilled out from the hotel room after them.

Joshua grabbed Vince's swinging right arm, twisting him and forcing his wrist up behind his back in a savage hammerlock.

Vince gave a yelp of pain. Joshua let him go and propelled him forward with a boot to the backside. Unfortunately, he misjudged the power of his kick and the stoutness of the hotel's carpentry.

Vince hurtled into the landing's balustrade. The

timber gave way with a splintering crash, and Vince went hurtling through to land with a sickening thump on the return flight of the staircase below.

Unable to check himself, he tumbled the rest of the way down. He bumped a different portion of his anatomy on each stair and he cursed a blue streak.

Bart Waller and Jake Phelps shoved past Joshua and bounded down the stairs two at a time to go to his assistance.

But the second Waller gunslick yelled, 'Gawd a'mighty!' And he went for his six-shooter.

4

THE BLOODSTAINED COAT

Joshua's wiry body moved with the smooth grace of a big cat. He hurled himself to one side and his Peacemaker cleared leather, flipped up.

Two shots smashed and echoed resoundingly up and down the passage and stairwell.

Joshua fired the fastest by a micro-second. He was also more or less accurate, which Waller's henchman wasn't, since his slug drilled into the ceiling, dislodging a shower of plaster on to his boss and his partner. Joshua hit the gunnie in the fleshy part of his left leg.

Nostrils flared, lips clamped in a steel-trap slit, the stricken man lowered himself to his knees, clutching the wound.

'Say a prayer; tighten it off with your belt before you bleed to death!' Joshua rapped.

The odds rapidly and unexpectedly reduced, Joshua kept the Peacemaker in his fist. Hotel staff and passing townsfolk were cautiously entering the lobby below, their curiosity sparked by the gunfire.

Joshua called down, 'You know what's best for him, you'll take your boy to Doc McAdams for an examination, Waller. Could be cracked bones. And send Phelps back up here. Your other trigger-happy hand has a slug in him for digging out and needs help to the medico likewise.'

The big, ambitious rancher looked up at him, eyes blazing. 'You ain't heard the last of this, Dillard! Nobody – but nobody – pushes the Wallers around. Consider due notice served!'

Waller ordered most of the gathering gawkers to scat, and he, his bruised son and his two gun-hands made a limping, less than dignified exit.

One spectator lingered, after circling the Waller party warily. Joshua recalled how he'd noticed him as one of the first arrivals. He had a dark, hawk face beneath a broad-brimmed, high-steepled sombrero. The rest of his duds were a hybrid of Mex *vaquero* and American cowboy. A brown-paper cigarette seemed stuck soggily to his lower lip.

'*Bueno*,' he said when Joshua descended the stairs. 'You a *pistolero*, huh? I like to see the Wallers take a beating.' His breath smelled sweetly of liquor. Tequila? Mescal?

'They got a price on your head, too?' Joshua asked.

'*Quien sabe, señor?*' he said laconically. 'I work for the Clamorgans. My name is Ramon Rubriz.'

39

'Ah . . . if I remember rightly, the Slash C *segundo.*'

The drooping cigarette and the smell of hard drink suggested infirmity of purpose, maybe lack of will-power, but a hooded hardness came to Rubriz's black agate eyes.

'No, I am Señora Clamorgan's *mayordomo,* the range boss. You see him on whom has fallen the unenviable responsibility to protect the Clamorgan rights and fortune.'

Joshua dipped his head. '*Pardona mi.* Permit me to introduce myself. I'm Joshua Dillard, a detective representing the father of Frank Clamorgan's fiancée. I'm here to discover what became of her in Welcome Valley. Tomorrow I'll ride out to the Slash C with Doctor McAdams to question Mrs Clamorgan.'

Rubriz's attitude changed; he bristled as though affronted.

'That should not be necessary, *amigo.* Slash C knows nothing about Señorita Greatheart's disappearance. Maybe you should pursue the Waller lice. The brat Vincent is a known womanizer.'

'So I hear. He may well tie in with this, and I aim to get around to looking into it. Point of fact, you could say the Wallers' attitude has me itching to start that particular ball rolling. Howsoever—'

'*Yuh know why I'm here, stranger?*'

A burly, bushy-browed man with a six-pointed star on his vest had bustled in to confront Joshua, who broke off at his curt interruption.

'Because there's been shooting, and a local bigwig has his nose out of joint some, I guess,' Joshua replied.

40

'Now don't misunnerstand me, I ain't sheddin' no tears over the Wallers, but I am askin' you to step along to my office, to give a sworn account of the whys and wherefores of the ruckus. As sheriff, thar's more gunnies than I can stomach runnin' loose in this county.'

'Mr Dillard is a detective, Señor Sherman,' Rubriz put in. 'I saw what he did. It was fortunate I have been in town with a buckboard to purchase tools. I will come, too – to hear what is said, to make a report. I am a witness in this.'

Sheriff Sherman raised a leery brow. 'Yuh got an interest here, Rubriz, aside of it bein' the Wallers that's inconvenienced? This man a stock detective yuh brought in?'

'I'm not a stock detective, Sheriff,' Joshua said.

'Oh, I thought yuh might-a been, Mr Dillard. The Slash C herds are kinda diminishin'. It's figgered bunches've been rustled and choused south by moonlight for sale to Mex bandits.'

'*Sí*, that, too, must be the Waller wolf-pack,' Rubriz said emphatically. 'Waller hires many that are owlhoots, trash. . . .'

'Yeah,' the tin-star said wearily. 'Some other time. Let's go take these affidavits.'

Joshua ruminated on the nuisance of the business, but in the event he managed to turn the unsought visit to the local law office to his own ends. Again he explained the purpose of his coming to Pike's Crossing and asked Sherman for his views on the mysterious disappearance of the girl from Denver.

'I would admire to help ol' Big Jack Greatheart,

him bein' a famous town-tamer an' all,' Sherman said, shaking his head. 'But it beats me an' a passel o' smarter brains. We got no evidence further'n a bloodstained coat, which on its lonesome is downright discouragin'. I'm sorry.'

'I'm sorry, too,' Joshua said, putting an edge on the words. 'Likewise Jack Greatheart.'

Horace Sherman's heavy frown cast a brooding shadow over his face. 'Ain't nothin' more a body can do, Dillard. The odds is plumb ag'inst yuh findin' Big Jack's gal alive – even dead – specially if powerful folks don't want her found.'

Joshua said, 'Do you still have the coat? I'd like to see it.'

'Sure. I ain't hidin' nothin', got no axes to grind. It's right here in the bottom drawer of this desk. Evidence that'll prob'ly never see no courtroom now, that's for sure.'

The macabre garment was produced. Joshua turned it over in his hands. The quilting was stiff with blood in several parts, though he noted it was not holed. Most significant were the smells – myriad and mingled – that clung to it.

Joshua was at once reminded of the reek of a slaughterhouse, but that might be a matter of association, brought about by the ominous stains. No, more predominant was a chemical whiff.

He sniffed at the jacket suspiciously.

'Do you keep chloroform in this office, Sheriff?' he asked.

Sherman was puzzled. 'What's that?'

'It's used medicinally to stupefy, render folk insensible. Midwives sometimes employ it. A Scotsman, a professor in Edinburgh, began the fashion, I believe. Queen Victoria had it when she gave birth the eighth time. She said it was soothing, quieting and delightful beyond all measure.'

'Naw, thar ain't no chloryform in Pike's Crossing.'

Ramon Rubriz stared, his dark eyes growing round as saucers.

'I understand the meaning of this, Señor Dillard, but there is an easy explanation. The jacket was kept some time at Doctor McAdams's house, which stinks to the high heaven of his gardenia toilet water and carbolic. That is what you smell.'

Joshua nodded. 'Oh, sure . . . now I place it. I've been in the medico's office and you're quite right. But what was the jacket doing there?'

Sheriff Sherman fidgeted uncomfortably. 'I put it up early when the find was fresh that the blood didn't 'xactly remind me of human blood, an' I seen some, Dillard. More like a cattle critter's. Doc kept it to take an expert look. He had it some weeks, then sent it back. Seems I might-a been mistook some. Yuh couldn't rightly tell.'

Joshua shot an accusing look at him. Investigation in Sherman's metropolis of the sagebrush was no better than Big Jack Greatheart had feared.

'So that was the end of it, huh?'

Sherman harrumphed. 'But about this shootin' at the Grand,' he said ponderously.

'In point of law,' Joshua said with more certainty than he felt, 'Waller's bunch was trespassing in my room. They started the rough-house stuff, fired the first shot, and got what they deserved.'

'*Sí*,' Rubriz put in eagerly. 'I believe in justice. It is time they have a lesson.'

'Well,' the sheriff said, 'I s'pose thar's no harm in speakin' ill of the livin', but of a nice dark night I'd watch your back from here on, Dillard. When his dander's up, Bart Waller an' his crowd don't mess none.'

Joshua said bitterly, 'Seems like this Waller has gotten you treed, Sheriff.'

'Waal . . . he's a big man with big ideas.'

' 'Specially around election time, I guess. A big, strong man to tell you what's right and what's wrong.'

'He has ambitious ideas for the valley, Dillard,' Sherman said defensively.

'Huh! I met too many men in the Pinks who knew what was politically best for everyone else. They only knew what was good for themselves, and that was seldom good for the little man. They promise you the world – but just hand over your independence and dignity.'

'It ain't like that,' Sherman protested.

But Joshua had turned his back and was walking out.

It was the brightest of Welcome Valley days. The sun, a fiery ball of white intensity, blazed down on the rich grasslands. It was a far piece from Sheriff Sherman's nice dark night, yet Joshua was mindful of the lawman's warning.

He'd bucked Bart Waller, the bull of the range. Waller and his reputedly evil son would want him put out of the way. The bushwhack route couldn't be discounted. It was plain Waller, embroiled in and crewed for his feud with the Slash C, had the men who might employ it – Jake Phelps and his gunslick cronies.

So as Joshua rolled over the range next morning with Doc McAdams in the medico's buggy, his eyes were peeled.

Cattle grazed in the hot sunshine. They were in prime condition, upgraded redbacks marked with the Slash C brand. The grass was plentiful and long and, with the space wide and open, showed little sign of trampling.

Joshua nodded his head in the beasts' direction. 'Good beef,' he observed to McAdams.

The saturnine doctor grunted, gloomy amid the brightness.

'But the herds have diminished in number since my old friend John Clamorgan's day,' he said sourly. 'Rustlers. The Waller outfit if I don't miss my guess.'

Joshua wondered if he couldn't somehow do something about that, even though his plate was full with tracing Emily Greatheart. Since leaving the Pinkerton agency, he'd been in essence a man with a burning sense of mission. As the Knights Templars of old had fought the Saracens, so he fought lawlessness in the Frontier West.

They skirted hill country – wild and broken, gashed by ravines and arroyos, spined by hogbacks and rocky ridges; exactly the kind of terrain where a drygulcher could safely lurk unseen till the last possible moment.

Joshua's attention was caught by an irregularity in the face of a steep slant. 'That the entrance to the abandoned mine?' he asked, pointing it out to McAdams.

'I do believe,' he said. 'The Spaniards hacked a shaft into the rock in their quest for precious metals. They worked the veins till there was no more yellow to be gouged out, or some say till they were massacred by Pima Indians.'

'Yeah, I hear say the place is haunted.'

'Tall tales abound, but the tunnel was walled up more than a century back. Frank Clamorgan figured to reopen it using modern methods to extract lead and appreciable silver, but since he was killed by the Wallers, all plans for boring have been put on hold. Augusta – Mrs Clamorgan leaves the running of the Slash C to Ramon Rubriz.'

The roadway bisected pleasant, undulating grassland but Joshua wasn't relaxed.

Alert though he was, when it came the sudden crack of a rifle was startling. It was followed on the instant by the snarling zip of a big-calibre slug past the back of his head.

Joshua was filled with fury over his vulnerability and the cowardliness of the attack. He swore.

'Missed, you gutless piece of shit!'

Doc McAdams gave a choking cry and pulled at the reins to halt his mare.

'No, keep moving, Doc!' Joshua commanded. 'They'll try another shot.'

But when the jittery McAdams whipped up the horse, he somehow managed to lose control of the light rig. It veered off the hard-packed trail and the nearside wheel slammed into a rock too big to miss. The wheel broke off the axle and the buggy lurched to a lopsided stop. Joshua leaped off the seat just as a second bullet screamed through the space where his head had been.

He rolled into a shallow drainage channel, roughly cut alongside the trail. The gunfire was coming from an overlooking, wooded slope, the perfect place for an ambusher.

Smoke emerged from a dark-green clump of mesquite trees, betraying the shooter's position. A nervous pair of quail rushed out from the ground growth – small, chunky, short-tailed and round-winged. The first bird was black with a chestnut crown; the second, probably the female, largely grey but with white-streaked chestnut flanks and a pale belly. Other birds were soaring above the trees' canopy, also crying protest.

Joshua wasn't the kind to play the part of a fish in a barrel. He'd prefer to die carrying the battle to his unseen assailant than wait to be picked off.

Drawing his Peacemaker with the cracked grip, he surged up and stormed the slope in a weaving run.

The trees were in a mass, their spreading, rounded crowns some twenty-five feet high. The trunks were thick with rough, dark brown bark shredding in strips. Yellowish-green flowers broke up the darker foliage, and the growth was armoured in places with stout yellow thorns.

Though he couldn't make out a target in the copse's denseness, Joshua fired into the clump as he ran toward it, knowing the hidden bushwhacker would realize he had him at a disadvantage if he gave him the time to figure it out.

Would his recklessness pay off or cost him his life?

5

'THINKING
I'M DEAD'

She was alone in a dark and musty place where time stood still. Or so it seemed. She had no timepiece to mark its passing, let alone real clothes. Left to her were just her undergarments, which were a camisole, a thin cotton petticoat and very plain drawers.

She was allowed a single candle to watch till it burned low and sometimes out, plunging her into the thick and frightening – the *total* – darkness before her jailers came to feed her and replace it.

Her prison had no windows and no sounds percolated its rough walls. It was a world of such silence it seemed to her the place must be underground, but this she didn't know because she'd been stupefied before they'd brought her here.

The earthy walls were shored by heavy timbers. The door was massive, appeared to be of iron and when it was opened, all she could glimpse beyond it was another door, a kind of double of the inner one.

Ventilation, though inadequate to disperse a permanent, rank mustiness was evidently via an iron-barred grating high up in a wall and beyond reach.

She could have languished here now for many weeks – in fact, her body had told she must have – but she had no other yardsticks against which she could reliably count the unwitnessed passing of days and nights. Meals appeared, irregularly she was sure, but she'd grown not to mind too much about the hunger pains till they were bad enough to make her weak and dizzy. For meals brought visits from her fiendish captors and tormentors, which she reckoned were best gone without.

To her persecutors she could give a number: three.

One took disgusting liberties with her. Lips curved in a little-boy smile, he touched her intimately, mocking her indignation and repeatedly threatening that next time he would come to rape her, but never quite committing the horrible crime that would irretrievably change her status in civilized, modern nineteenth-century society – were she allowed to return to it.

The second leering persecutor reviled her – spitting, pulling her by the hair and prodding her cruelly in places that hurt. Driven by the furies of jealousy perhaps. She could still hear in her head the second's description of the first: 'He is a hound in the first degree!'

The third was worst of all – crushingly accusing

her of exerting a corrupting influence, of flaunting her charms, of being immodest and deviant, and promising she would be required before she died to do all kinds of shocking penance in answer to the dreadful and untrue charges.

She shuddered at the horrors of her incarceration.

But she had to be brave. Wasn't she still Emily Greatheart, the daughter of Big Jack Greatheart, former frontier marshal – a bold, fighting man who'd bested the dregs of the Wild West and brought law and order to some of the unruliest towns ever established in the whole of America? 'Raggedy-assed, terrible places,' she'd been told.

She forced herself to think of pleasant things. Of blue skies and green grass. Of flowers and trees and the breeze in your face. Of dear ones, like her dad. . . .

No, that was not a good idea. She immediately pictured him alone in his bed in Denver, fretting at her prolonged absence, possibly giving up all hope of their reunion, and knowing he was frustratingly help-less to find and save her.

'*Thinking I'm dead.*'

The unbidden, unstoppable tears moistened her eyes as she breathed the words into the thick, palpable silence. She thought her very name a bitter irony; maybe her heart would break before she could escape this place.

Joshua heard the crash of breaking stems. The bush-whacker was retreating through the tangled stand of mesquite in the face of his determined attack. The intended victim (himself) had turned aggressor. It was how Joshua wanted it to be, but he didn't mean to let the murderous scoundrel to escape.

He snarled, 'I'm coming in there after you, sonofabitch!'

He came to the sniper's nest – a flattened area, littered with brass shell casings glinting dully, but vacated in haste and possible panic.

The thicket didn't afford easy passage. Every part of the mesquite was covered in short, dense hairs and the fern-like dark-green leaves were divided into many tiny leaflets. Most disconcertingly, the branches that supported it all were prickly with stout, yellow thorns. Some of the spikes were more than an inch long, hooked and wicked.

Cussing the impediments to his progress, Joshua forged on, tagging and ripping his clothes in his determined haste. A flock of thrashers that had possibly been nesting in the trees' canopy continued to whirl and scream overhead.

He saw the bulk of a moving shape ahead. His scratched face was stony and bleak as he raised the Peacemaker and squeezed the trigger twice, stabbing his shots at the vague, obscured target.

A flash split the shadows as his quarry returned the fire, but fortunately missed.

Joshua fired again. This time shots came from both guns, and the bushwacker's bullet thudded into the wide trunk of a tree where Joshua had sought cover. Pieces of shaggy bark flew into his eyes, temporarily blinding him.

By the time he'd wiped them out, and his vision

was cleared of tears, his attacker had broken free to a horse tethered on the outer reaches of the woodland. Through the tangled brush, Joshua caught only a glimpse of the man, dappled by shadows, vaulting into the saddle. The thwarted attacker instantly spurred his snorting mount into a leaping start.

The animal was no dead head or stick horse, but a top bronc that took off out of the mesquite split-seconds after its rider was astride. More of the woodland was smashed and crushed under sure hoofs.

Joshua plunged after his enemy on foot, but by the time he was clear of the trees, the horse, a big bay, was well away and stretched out in a flowing run.

'High-tailed it, damnit!'

The rider was crouched low over the horse's neck and bare-headed. Joshua's smarting eyes were doubly afflicted by emergence into the bright sunlight. Dust puffed like a smokescreen from under the pounding hoofs. Joshua made out only that the man wore common range garb. Briefly, he wondered whether an identifying factor might be that this would now be as thorn-clawed as his own clothing, though it wasn't possible to be sure of even that.

He searched for other, accessible clues to the person who'd attempted his murder.

'The low-down drygulcher!' he muttered. He could take a good guess at who wanted him dead in this country, but his Pinkerton experience had taught him never to bypass potential evidence.

On the edge of the thicket, he found tell-tale hoof-prints in softer soil shaded by the trees' canopy. He knelt and examined them closely. A grunt of satisfaction escaped his pursed lips. The embedded marks told his practised eyes the bay horse had a worn shoe on the nearside foreleg. He would watch out for such a horse, and woe betide its owner!

He straightened up and trudged back to the wrecked buggy, still full of wrath.

McAdams was waiting for him, full of visible apprehension at odds with his customary air of resigned gloom.

'The buggy's useless,' he said dourly. 'That wheel's not only off – the rim's cracked, but the mare is broken to the saddle. Maybe we should return forthwith to Pike's Crossing.'

Joshua saw he'd already unhitched the horse.

'Maybe we shouldn't,' he said flatly. 'Don't like to contradict, Doc, but I don't see why some unsuccessful sharp-shooter, prob'ly out to murder for a cash bonus, should change a day's plans.'

McAdams was huffy. 'What do you suggest then, Mr Dillard?'

'We ride on double to the Slash C. We complete our business. Then Mrs Clamorgan can loan me a mount to return to Pike's Crossing.'

'A plague on Waller gunmen!' McAdams said, showing heat. 'Supposing they make another attempt on our lives?'

'Reckon it's me they're after,' Joshua said dryly. 'I'm prepared to take the risk. Somehow I don't see 'em having a second ambush set up.'

But McAdams hadn't done bellyaching. 'That's all very well in theory, but I'm not a gunfighter, Mr

Dillard. Your attitude could have us both dead and gone.'

Joshua wasn't persuaded to turn tail.

'Trust me, Doc. I know lawbreakers – hate 'em, but know 'em. Brand-blotters, road agents, bank robbers, train robbers, claim jumpers ... all kinds of trail trash. I've faced 'em down and shot it out with the very worst. Most of the cheats and the killers are dead. I'm not.'

McAdams said unhappily, 'I've heard about your unrelenting ferocity, Dillard. Myself, I would prefer caution.'

The Slash C headquarters was arranged along lines Joshua had seen all over the South-west. The layout had plainly been set by original Mexican owners.

Adobe-and-log ranch buildings were grouped around a large treed yard. Dominating the scene was a fine main house with porticoed verandas and a red tile roof.

The place might strike the unsavvy visitor as being more like a small village or mission than a ranching family's home lot. For a fact, Joshua recognized that the prettiest structure, painted white and complete with a bell tower, must once have been an old church. Beneath the gleaming, lime-based whitewash was what looked like fired brick, dressed with stone and ornate plaster scrollwork.

'That's some edifice,' Joshua said. 'It still used as a church?'

McAdams said stiffly, 'It was built in the 1700s for two Franciscan friars, Juan Espinosa and Felipe

Cordova, in the Spanish colonial style. It's now Mrs Clamorgan's private chapel. Frank Clamorgan is entombed in its crypt and she spends long hours there at her prayers. She was a very devoted mother, especially after the passing of Frank's pa, my good friend John.'

Joshua thought it was probably a pleasant enough place to take your grief and an inspiring piece of architecture. The same couldn't be said for all the buildings. The ugliest erection, set well apart, was a thick-walled, stone-and-adobe rectangle. To avoid comment on Augusta Clamorgan's morbid pastime, he asked what it might be.

'That's the powderhouse where explosives were stored for use in the mine,' McAdams said. 'Young Frank was going to put it to use again when his mine machinery arrived from Denver.'

Despite the large network of corrals, an eerie aura of inactivity hung over the extensive property. No one rushed to greet them or to inquire about the unseemly nature of their arrival on single, unsaddled horseback. The few men who moved about the place evidently unsupervised were Mexicans in broad-brimmed sombreros, loose white cotton pants and flapping shirts.

'*Buenas días, amigos,*' Joshua called, but some simply froze, staring, and others were disinterested.

Joshua squinted at the sun. Noon was only an hour or so away, so perhaps the ruling torpidity wasn't to be wondered at; the people were readying themselves for the heat.

They climbed down in the cool shade of a huge

mariposa tree with bell-shaped orange flowers, which Joshua guessed was a welcome itself of sorts in the absence of any other. McAdams lifted the iron latch of a yard gate and they tramped up the walk to the porch and main door of the *hacienda*.

The oaken door was heavy, strapped with black iron and with hinges of the same. But the most striking feature was a decaying memorial wreath. Tacked to the door, dried brown and crumbling, it had plainly been there months.

'A tribute to Frank,' McAdams explained. 'The Clamorgan household remains in mourning.'

Joshua shook his head, filled with disbelief, and the emblem didn't stop him hammering on the door with a solid fist. McAdams flinched at the hollow din.

'Have a care for civility, Dillard!'

When the door was swung open in answer it was by a woman of Mexican ancestry. She blinked dark eyes as though in surprise.

McAdams treated her to a courteous dip of his head, but appeared guarded. '*Buenas días. . . .*'

A housekeeper of some kind, Joshua thought, and that might be the role she filled, but McAdams introduced her as Señora Francisca Rubriz, wife of range-boss Ramon.

She could have been beautiful except for what Joshua instantly categorized as a feline hardness. About thirty years of age, she had a full, coming on heavy figure. She was dark-haired, dark-eyed and dark olive-skinned, with an oval-shaped face and small ears. She wore a dowdy black dress and her only adornment was a thick gold wedding band on her finger.

Joshua imagined that a few years earlier, with a smile and some bright ribbons in braided hair, she would have been a voluptuous, head-turning beauty.

She appeared startled to see them, but the look was fleeting, replaced by a hostile sullenness.

'Why are you here?' she rasped petulantly in a harsh, Mexican-accented voice.

'It's Wednesday, Señora Rubriz,' McAdams said, as though enunciating the situation for an idiot. 'I always see Mrs Clamorgan on Wednesdays.'

Joshua said, 'I thought word had been sent by your husband that I'd accompany the doctor.'

Francisca Rubriz shrugged. '*Quién sabe?* I don't know what is going on now. Do you, Doctor?'

McAdams could be belligerently blunt, too. 'Can't say as I do anymore. But you are Mrs Clamorgan's housekeeper and insolence ill-behooves you. Mr Dillard has matters to discuss with your mistress.'

The woman's response was close to a hiss.

'*Sí*, I understand, Doctor, but you of all people know how it is, eh? Señora Clamorgan has secluded herself privately in the chapel, as is her way. She says endless prayers to God for her murdered son. The whims of the *señora* are inconvenient ... *hacer un gran daño* ... but we have to live with them. And they come between me and my Ramon—'

'Enough!' McAdams barked. 'We'll listen to no disrespect or tale-telling.'

'Pah! Are you like the Indians, Doctor McAdams, to think a woman is fit only to make meals, gather wood, fetch water, warm a bed?'

Joshua fumed at the stupidity of the further delay.

'Señora, we came to visit with Mrs Clamorgan,' he said tensely. 'It's been none too easy getting here, and I'm going to see it happens.'

Grim-faced, he swung on his heel from her bitter passion and went in raking strides toward the alien tranquillity of the chapel.

6

LADY IN BLACK

Joshua was prepared to find the interior of the Spanish-looking chapel a picture of Roman Catholic sumptuousness and elegance. But he found it somewhat removed from anything he'd expected.

Across the Border, Joshua had been in like places that were treasure houses of statuary and plate; precious-metal gew-gaws inviting plunder. And sure, some of this small church's luxurious style had been preserved.

The plasterwork of the high ceiling was intricate. Heavy red tapestry looked dusty but was still rich in colour, as were stained timbers. The floor had alternate black-and-white paving stones – just like an outsize board for checkers, Joshua thought irreverently. The gloomy shadows were interspersed by soft, shifting pools of light created by candles in gilt holders. The candles – exceptionally, expensively tall – flickered and sometimes emitted wispy coils of oily black smoke.

But all the pews had been removed and the main floor was dominated by a railed-off altar.

A tall woman in a black gown and with a black shawl draped from her head kneeled on a hassock before the altar with her back to the door.

Joshua hailed her inquiringly. 'Mrs Augusta Clamorgan?'

Despite his gentle tone, she started. When she rose to her feet and turned, she showed a lined, haggard face, pale but blotched with blazing anger, and lit by eyes that glittered from dark hollows.

In a fierce, croaking voice that put Joshua in mind of an evil bird with black plumage, she said, 'How dare you intrude on my devotions!'

Joshua kept his own rising gorge in check.

'I'm Joshua Dillard. It was my understanding you'd agreed to receive me this morning to discuss the disappearance of the daughter of my client, ex-Marshal Jack Greatheart, of Denver.'

'Ah, Mr Dillard, is it?' she said, her tongue no less sharp for his stating of his business. 'Well, the name Greatheart is an anathema to me! I wish Miss Emily Greatheart had never entered my dear son's life. Then he might be with us today instead of in the hereafter.'

'I don't follow. It could equally be said if your son hadn't entered Emily's life, Mr Greatheart mightn't be missing his daughter. Can't you imagine how he feels?'

Measured footsteps behind Joshua told him McAdams had followed him into the church.

'Have a care, Dillard!' the medico warned. 'Your rude haste is liable to upset my patient.'

Joshua muttered, 'No more'n her one-sided attitude is already upsetting me.'

McAdams rejoined, 'It has been noted you've an abrasive manner and an uncertain temper, sir.'

Joshua's jaw tightened. 'I'm beginning to see why the local lawdogs gave up the trail.'

Augusta Clamorgan said shrilly, 'If you want to hound anyone, Mr Dillard, hound the killer of my son. Bring Vincent Waller to justice and a hangman's noose!'

'Maybe that's exactly what I'll have to do when I find out what's become of Big Jack Greatheart's girl.'

'Greatheart! Greatheart! I'm under no obligation to answer the man's ridiculous letters – or pestering questions from his agent.'

Augusta was uncompromising. 'My son was killed in a petty dispute over his daughter's likeness. If she'd never wheedled her way into his affections, that wouldn't have happened.'

'You might be a grieving mother, Mrs Clamorgan, but you have a stony heart.'

McAdams touched Joshua's sleeve restrainingly. 'That's quite enough, Dillard.'

Joshua brushed him off; the medico was turning into some kind of gadfly nuisance. 'Don't need any handler, Doc.'

McAdams was dancing attendance to a rich and powerful client – his old friend's widow. It seemed to Joshua he was prepared by his intervention to block the questioning – to endorse the bizarre position she took – in a sickeningly sycophantic way.

The hell with that! Trying a new line, Joshua said, 'Mrs Clamorgan, after Emily Greatheart came to visit with you, she didn't return to Pike's Crossing. Do you believe she was waylaid by the man who killed your son? Him or his father's roughnecks?'

And this time, maybe Joshua had got through to her warped mind. She appeared to ponder the question, her mad eyes staring fixedly across the empty church into middle distance.

Into the vacuum of the pause dropped the sound of the hot breeze sighing fitfully through the open door and stirring the leaves of the mariposa in the yard outside. But that wasn't all. Joshua froze and held his breath, listening intently for a repeat of another, less explicable sound.

Augusta said abruptly, 'The Rocking W Cattle Company is a company of bandits! Waller hires wolves good for nothing outside of killing the innocent, swilling liquor and seeking the favours of bawds. The devil's crew!'

Joshua nodded. Now he was getting somewhere. 'Did Emily say anything about the Wallers to you? Had they approached her in Pike's Crossing perhaps?'

'Not that she *said*. But they would have all figured on getting at her. Hadn't they cast hungry eyes over her provoking picture? A flighty city gal dressed for some grand ballroom! Doubtless Vincent Waller, a known womanizer, would have marked a fancy woman like her for himself.'

Joshua frowned. 'Fancy woman?'

'Oh yes. She had to be one of the Jezebel breed. No lily. She tempted my Frank, didn't she? It was because of her he was shot dead!'

Astounded by the claim, which was balder than anything she'd said previously, Joshua said, 'How can you make such extravagant charges? D'you have no care at all for Miss Greatheart or her father?'

She said unequivocally, her voice cracking with emotion, 'I don't give a damn for any has-been town-tamer or his scheming flirt of a daughter! I've been deprived of my *son*!'

She turned her back on Joshua and kneeled again before the altar. For the first time Joshua noticed a gilt-framed picture surmounted it. It showed a slimly built young man, fair-haired and good-looking.

Joshua stepped closer and was not surprised to see 'Frank Clamorgan' engraved in flowing script on a small panel at the base of the frame. What did surprise him – shock him – was the pallid look he detected in the subject's eyes and a looseness of his full-lipped mouth. Though plainly revered by Augusta Clamorgan, the picture suggested to Joshua viciousness and an instability of character.

Had the Wallers been right in their dismissive assessment of the dead Clamorgan heir? Had Big Jack Greatheart's girl made a mistake in accepting him as her beau and husband-to-be?

Again, Joshua heard the odd sound. It was a rustling, struggling noise, out of place and originating from somewhere the half-empty church's hollow acoustics didn't allow him to pinpoint. Did it come from under his feet – a crypt? From over his head – the roof?

He tensed, but when the sound was quickly lost, he gave a mental shrug. Probably it was one of the creaks older buildings made when their dry timbers baked in the sun, like the rheumatic bones of an old man easing himself into some new, less stressful position.

McAdams said, 'I think we should leave, Dillard.'

'Yes!' Augusta croaked. 'You're disturbing me, Mr Dillard. Please go!'

Joshua felt sorry for her, but he was more sorry for Jack Greatheart, and he had to know.

'One last time,' he persisted. 'You met Emily just before she disappeared. Did she—?'

'There is nothing I can tell you that I haven't!' she blurted. 'The county's peace officers have declared the fool girl missing, presumed dead.'

'Come!' McAdams said, tugging his arm. 'We're wasting our time, man, and distressing a sick woman.'

This time Joshua didn't shake the medico off. He was right in the first part, since it had proved impossible to make headway against the woman's closed mind, though he deplored the encouragement McAdams had given her with his solicitude. Under the circumstances, McAdams was taking protection of a patient to remarkable lengths.

And it came a third time. As Joshua made for the door in hostile silence, he heard it. There was a sound! A sound that didn't belong in the church. He strained every nerve to catch it properly.

'For God's sake, what *is* it? That muffled pattering?'

McAdams ground out a reprimand before he gave Joshua the answer.

'You shouldn't take the Lord's name in vain in his own house, Dillard. . . . But it's pigeons. Just pigeons nesting in the bell tower is all.'

In the candle-lit gloom of her prison, Emily Greatheart stopped the pacing that was her only exercise. Her alarmed gaze turned to the solid door. It was opening on groaning hinges.

Which of her fiendish jailers would this be?

Once, she'd tried to bar entry, leaning her weight against the door, but the man had shoved back and jammed his foot in the opening. When she'd finally been forced to relax, he'd surged in, hurling her across the chamber. She hadn't tried that desperate ploy again. She'd also been given the grim warning that she could starve to death if she chose.

The same man came in now, a grin on his face. He was empty-handed, this time bringing her no food or drink. She knew from the grin that he'd come for sport.

She said in a dry-mouthed voice that shook, 'Leave me alone! Get out of here! I told you to keep away from me! I'll tell the others!'

But he kicked the door shut behind him and advanced on her like a cat cornering a mouse, antic-ipating his pleasure. She smelled sweat on him – his own and that of a hard-ridden horse. He laughed evilly.

'I think it's time I take some fun. I deserve it – a reward for effort one might say.'

'What effort have you made?' she demanded shakily.

'A range dick has been sent by your father, but he has been led a fine dance! I spit at him.'

Emily's heart leaped with sudden hope. 'If you were honourable, you'd take my part, release me from this hell and let me go to this man. I'd do anything for you then. I'd say nothing of what you've done. You can trust me. . . .'

'I trust no one,' he jeered. 'Not even my own grandmother, and certainly you are not her!'

'Give me back my clothes! I want to go back to Denver. The detective will take me to my father. No complaint will be laid.'

The answer was scornful. 'Your clothes have been burned and the dick will be lucky to leave the country with his own life!'

He came toward her, looming and threatening in the flickering half-light of the guttering candle. The tightness in her throat grew till she thought it would choke her.

'Touch me and you'll be made to pay!' she managed jerkily.

'No, *you* are going to pay. I will take payment in full for all that is owed me. I have you at my mercy. You can cry rape and murder to bring the others running about my ears, but no one will hear you from here.'

'But they'll find out. Everyone will find out one day!'

'Horse chips! Why so any mystery in this border territory about a girl with your looks and charm vanishing somewhere along a lonely trail – especially when there are so many bad and desperate characters about? Your disappearance will never be pinned on us.'

He reached out for her and she screamed, 'No! Please – please no!'

He took no notice. His rough, strong hands seized her, and she struggled with him but knew the fight was lost before it was begun.

He laughed in her burning face. 'Be nice to me or it'll be the worse for you!'

'You daren't—'

He brought a hand up and slapped her hard across the cheeks, both ways.

Silenced and stunned, she drew breath and let it out in a great sob.

He kissed her, holding her head, his mouth hard on hers. She tried to resist, beating at his back with clenched fists, but she was powerless to stop him. His mouth tore at her lips, again and again. Then he picked her up effortlessly and threw her on the crude, iron-framed bunk with its musty straw palliasse.

'Give you clothes?' he mocked. 'Better we begin with you having no clothes, I think!'

He hooked a hand through the loops of the pink ribbon laced through the front of her camisole and tugged mightily. Once. Twice. The third time, eyelets and seams were torn from the fabric and the garment peeled free from the swells of her bosom.

'Oh, God!' she cried, shuddering, trying to cover herself with her hands.

Then he was ripping her petticoat. She screamed again and again, and her senses reeled blackly as she was struck by the full horror of what was about to happen to her.

7

KING RAT

Hunches were part of Joshua Dillard's stock-in-trade. They didn't, he thought, cost him anything. With a purse apt to be depleted as often as Joshua's this was a worthy consideration. Too bad it wasn't always right, and that complete luck was seldom his trail partner.

With his Slash C inquiries in the company of Doctor McAdams thwarted, Joshua left the Clamorgan *hacienda* on a begrudgingly loaned mount. A short distance past the spot on the road where they'd been ambushed, he reached a fork that hadn't been as obvious when they'd been heading in the opposite direction on the way out from Pike's Crossing.

He halted the borrowed horse, narrowed his eyes against the glare of the noonday sun and studied the country all about. The side trail headed westward, climbing into the more broken, higher land that contained the old mine Frank Clamorgan had made his last interest in life before meeting Emily Greatheart.

For no particularly convincing reason, Joshua decided to scout out this piece of landscape. It didn't seem totally outside the bounds of feasibility that Frank's fiancée might have made a similar decision to detour on her ill-fated buggy ride back from the Slash C, though Sheriff Sherman's trackers had evidently found no sign to support the conjecture.

What could have been more natural than for Emily to want to sight at closer quarters the mine that had brought Frank to Denver and into her life?

The branch trail climbed into the hilly stuff by way of the more accessible, barer ridges, but it also presented choices. Here and there, older sections wended through arroyos now overgrown with trees but maybe still passable to those in the know and who preferred to make their way less openly.

Could be I've been reading too many penny-dreadfuls, Joshua chastised himself silently at this last thought. Why would anyone want to sneak up to a mine that was closed and all but worthless to a casual prospector?

One answer that came to him – the most fantastic anyone would be likely to think of – was character-ized by audacity so extreme it had to be a result of wishful thinking.

What if Emily Greatheart was still alive, kept pris-oner in some isolated place, like the abandoned Spanish mine?

For a band of dyed-in-the-wool ruffians, like Bart

Waller's, a woman had only one meaning, one purpose. In a secret place, they could use her over and over for their disgusting pleasure till the rigours and the exhaustion of it took an inevitable toll. Flesh and mind could endure only so much.

He pushed the Slash C horse up a steep, almost perpendicular slope. His mind was busy with the possibilities. He began considering the number of weeks since Emily had gone missing and a cold and ruthless anger over the imagined ordeal took hold of him, making him careless of his own safety in a country where he'd been threatened and shot at.

Joshua topped out on the barren rim of an arroyo which had trees growing in it. And his eyes gleamed.

'By God,' he breathed softly, 'I do believe someone is down there!'

The ugly croaks of a toad, irregularly spaced, hinted at water under the shade of the shaggy trees, and the prolific green growth itself was a confirming indicator; if water wasn't on the surface, then it was down below a near piece. Also, what else would a man and a horse be doing, loitering among the trees, other than watering?

The horse was a calico, which was a small disappointment, since Joshua had a strong desire to meet up with the man on the bay who'd tried to bushwhack him.

The morning's gunplay in the mesquite clump had left Joshua short on fresh loads for his Peacemaker, so despite the supposition that the lurking rider was up to no good in this neck of the woods, he decided an armed challenge would be a mistake.

Moreover, if the man was a desperado of some stripe, as was likely, it would surely come to shooting and either of them could end up dead. Which wouldn't serve his purpose, or that of the stricken man in Denver who'd hired him.

Joshua meant to find out the unknown's business in the lonely spot, and there was only one way to do it. The sonofabitch would have to tell him. And as they said, dead men told no tales.

He dismounted and left his horse on dropped reins. He figured his inquiries might eventually produce an open clash, but he clambered down into the brush- and tree-choked arroyo with the stealth of a stalker.

The man and horse were in a small, circular clearing. The man was filling a big rawhide canteen at a waterhole. Joshua made two immediate, significant discoveries. The man was no unknown. He was the Waller hand Jake Phelps – the bulky one with the incongruous physiognomy of a rat.

The other finding was a mound of rocks in the clearing's centre: a wilderness grave.

Joshua trod warily toward Phelps, digesting his observations. How did he tackle the approach now? After the fight at the Grand Hotel in Pike's Crossing, Phelps would be hostile for sure.

Having the drop on him, Joshua began to ease his .45 from his holster. But it all fell apart sooner than he bargained. Up on the rim, the Slash C horse nickered.

Phelps's calico raised its head instantly, ears twitching. Before it could answer the other horse, Phelps

73

span round in a flowing movement, quicksilver-fast, and hurled the filled canteen at Joshua.

Instead of continuing his draw, cocking and firing, Joshua instinctively raised his arm to fend off the heavy object. Then Phelps was on him in a rush, his narrow, rat face twisted in a dark snarl, the eyes narrowed to slits.

'Dillard! I'll smash yuh plumb to bits!'

Phelps crashed into Joshua with breathtaking force, fists flailing.

Joshua was flung backwards on tottering feet, his gun hand hovering again over the black-gripped butt of his Peacemaker, but not reaching it.

Phelps had big, hard fists and the power behind them was deceptively enormous. He kept on coming, landing more punishing blows, almost as though he'd been ready and primed for the encounter.

With a roar of rage, Joshua struck back. He landed a quick, short-arm jab into Phelps's snarling face and had the pleasure of seeing the punch split his upper lip.

Momentarily, Phelps reeled, dashing away the sudden welling of blood. But he was rawhide-tough and leapt back in, making no move to go for a gun, still determined to smash Joshua 'to bits'.

'Yuh got this owing from the Rockin' W, mister!' he said thickly.

There, it was said. Phelps was out to avenge the drubbing Joshua had dealt the deputation that had come to warn him off in Pike's Crossing. Big Bart Waller had said, '*Nobody – but nobody – pushes the Wallers around. Consider due notice served*!' Here was the meanest of the hardcases on the cattleman's payroll, paid top dollar for other than range-riding skills, dishing it out.

If he faltered now, Joshua knew he'd be destroyed.

As Phelps waded in with windmilling fists, Joshua ducked under an oncoming blow and put a fist explosively into Phelps's middle. Breath and gas belched from his bleeding mouth.

But the king rat wasn't beaten. He snatched with both hands at Joshua's throat, his aim to keep close, reducing the velocity of repeat body jabs . . . and to throttle the life from the accursed range dick!

They were struggling toe to toe, two powerful men, both intent on downing the other.

Joshua knew enough of rough-house fighting to know there were no rules to break, only Phelps's hold and the stalemate they'd fought to.

He kneed Phelps in the groin, ruthlessly.

Phelps lost his stranglehold and sagged forward, face gone sickly grey, but wrapping himself smotheringly around Joshua, and turning his hip to protect his throbbingly bruised parts. He mauled. He clawed at Joshua's face trying to get his thumbs in his eyes, all the time regaining his gasping breath.

Joshua was battered and his face bloodied by the raking claws that were Phelps's nails. It seemed to him they'd already been fighting for hours in a strained silence broken only by the meaty thump of bare knuckles on facial flesh and bone, and by grunts of extreme pain.

It was time for Joshua to try bluff. In a daring, odds-against gamble that might leave him crippled for life, he dropped his defences and let himself go limp with a sob of despair, as though he was out of strength, all-in.

Phelps fuelled a yell of victory with panting breath and squared up to carry out his threat to smash Joshua. He almost tore the shirt from his back as he hauled him upright to deliver the killing, sledge-hammer blow.

That was when Joshua stiffened, stepped in close and, gritting his teeth, rammed up his knee again.

'Suckered by the same trick twice, Phelps,' he said.

This time they crashed together to the ground, rolling in a continued struggle to gain mastery. But Phelps was in agony as the fire from his crotch spread paralysingly through his hard body, and Joshua came out on top.

Joshua had Phelps pinned between his knees. He drew his long-barrelled Peacemaker and stuck the muzzle into the tough's sweat-slickened forehead so hard it made an indentation.

'You're going to talk, Phelps! Where's your boss's son taken Emily Greatheart? Is she in that goddamned grave over there?'

Despite his painful situation, Phelps grinned. 'Wouldn't yuh like to know, Mr Clever Dick!'

Joshua felt an almost uncontrollable urge to put a slug through the sneering man's brains, but he repressed it, scowling.

'You'd better spill the beans fast, Phelps.' He raked the gun's sight across the thug's cheek and the blood flowed some more from his torn lip.

'Naw! She ain't in the grave. That's a Mex rustler –

one o' the bunch that c'llects the rustled Slash C an' other stock fer takin' 'cross the border.'

'And you and your thieving crowd would know all about that, wouldn't you? Seeing as you run off the beeves in the first place!'

'Think yuh know it all, Dillard, doncha?' Phelps retorted surlily. 'Even that ain't as plain as it looks.'

'Huh! It's plain enough. If it was Rocking W stock going missing, Bart Waller would make it a hanging matter. So what was this? A warning to an accomplice who got too big for his boots?'

'Can't say.'

'No nevermind. It isn't what concerns me here. The question I'm putting is where has Vince Waller hidden Emily Greatheart? Has he got her holed up in the old mine? Is that it?'

The dark rat eyes glittered in their slits. 'Yeah, that's right. Thar's ways inta that mine. Vince's got a hideout. I'll take yuh, Dillard. I ain't takin' no more o' this. Top Waller dinero ain't all by a long sight.'

'Fine. I'll let you up and you take me,' Joshua said, his voice hard.

The tip of Jake Phelps tongue crept out to lick at spilled blood. 'Make sure yuh don't drill me with your blasted Peacemaker, Dillard.'

'I'm not going to kill you, less you try to trick me.'

'Listen,' Phelps pleaded, 'I ain't huntin' no more trouble with yuh. I reck'n yuh're loco.'

Joshua lifted off him. 'Sure I'm loco . . . in behalf of a sick old man in Denver who wants his daughter back. Now get up!'

Phelps said truculently, 'Anyhow, swear to God

yuh'd never find your own way into the mine if'n yuh killed me.' He got to his feet unsteadily.

'Mebbe not, though I figure any swearing you do ain't worth a damn. Hoist your hands!'

Joshua lifted the gunslick's sidearm from the tied-down, greased holster and threw it in the bushes beyond the ominous grave of the alleged Mexican receiver of stolen cattle.

'Hey, that was a good gun!'

'With the money Waller pays you to wet-nurse his brattish son you can buy another. To the mine!'

They trudged up from the arroyo. With Joshua close behind, Phelps led the way to the mine, then went past the wall of rocks that blocked the entrance to the main shaft, stumbling over hacked and sun- and wind-weathered detritus.

Joshua saw a cluster of anaemic scrub trees higher up amid a jumble of boulders, some several feet in girth and height. It was toward these Phelps headed. He pointed.

'Up there. Vince found another way in covered by the trees.'

They scrambled up a talus slope. Joshua could feel sweat beginning to prickle the back of his neck, and it wasn't from the heat of the day or his exertions in the fight.

Phelps said, 'Ain't no more'n a bitsy fissure. Yuh'll have to stoop.'

'Vince Waller's no jackrabbit. If he can get a kidnapped girl through this hole in the ground, we can make it, too.'

Phelps entered first. 'Mind, I ain't 'xactly said

yuh'll find no lawdog's li'le gal – jest that Vince has been rootin' roundabout since the Clamorgan kid cashed his chips.'

Inside, the tunnel quickly widened, but took a curve that would cut off the daylight.

When Joshua, hesitating, saw Phelps's broken lip lift off his front teeth in a sudden grin, yellowy-white in the gloom, it was already too late.

He heard the gritty scrape of boot leather in a black aperture alongside him. He heard the swish of something heavy falling.

As he started to twist around, the iron of a gun thudded against the side of his head, over his left ear. His senses exploded in a blinding flash. The Peacemaker dropped from his nerveless fingers. He felt his legs fold up under him and the hard floor of the tunnel came up and hit him in the face.

8

'PIG OF A DIFFERENT BRISTLE'

Joshua came to his senses on a dirt floor in a lamplit cavern. Around him and above him were stoutly shored walls and ceiling. Close by was a cluster of old and rotting digging tools, left perhaps by the Mexicans who'd worked the mine in the century prior.

Phelps awaited his return to consciousness with three others. Two were of the same ilk – Anglo border trash, gunslicks of the kind engaged by an ambitious cattleman expanding his empire in a valley where grass was abundant but where only one man could be monarch.

The third man was the cattleman's son, Vincent Waller, smirkingly pleased with himself. He had a pair of field-glasses slung from his neck by a strap.

Joshua groaned deliberately and let his eyes close. The longer he could keep realization of his full consciousness from his captors the better.

'Damnit, Vince, this game's gone fur enough,' Phelps said.

'Hold it, Jake,' Vince rapped. 'What are you figuring to do with that Peacemaker?'

'Whadyuh think?' Phelps replied harshly. 'Meltin' a hogleg over his pate ain't near fittin' – put one o' his own slugs through his brains is all.'

'No you're not. I ain't had *my* fun yet. You don't do as I say, I'll tell Pa. I do that and you'll be told to roll your bed and hit the trail.'

'Jesus, Vince, I'd like fer yuh to know it weren't easy trickin' him inta here.'

'So? You agreed to lure him on, didn't you? When I saw him afore noon through the field-glasses with that fool McAdams, he pointed over here. After that, it was a fair bet the ex-Pink'd come snooping around Hell's Half Acre on account of the Clamorgan kid's interest in the mine.'

'Mebbe so, Vince, but—'

'No buts! You jumped at the chance to teach him a lesson, and I'm glad we had a back-up plan to fix the bastard. Just 'cause he got the better of you when you chose to fight, don't make it a pig of a different bristle.'

Phelps was peeved and made a growling noise. 'He's in no shape to give yuh no fun, Vince.'

The younger man stepped forward and kicked Joshua brutally in the side.

'We'll see about that. Geddup, Dillard!'

Joshua was waiting for him and this was the best chance he'd been given so far. It might be his last. Swivelling on to his buttocks, he thrust out and up suddenly with his booted feet.

'You're not the only one can kick, Waller!'

Vince took the full force of the mighty, stiff-legged kick in the chest. He was catapulted backwards into his three cronies and they went down in a cursing heap. Phelps dropped the Peacemaker.

Joshua grabbed up an ancient pick and swung wildly. But the wooden handle was worm-eaten. The implement's rusty iron head hurtled off, and hit the rock wall ringingly, high up. Speed unchecked, the lethal chunk of heavy iron came down so that a wicked spike plunged full into the chest of one of the sprawled hardcases.

The unfortunate vented one last chilling scream before the blood flooded his punctured lung and bubbled from his mouth.

Luck for once had been squarely on Joshua's side.

He took off in the stunned hiatus, pausing only to stoop and scoop up his trusty old Colt. Someone had set hand-rails into both walls of the tunnel leading from the cavern. Once the light from the lamps was behind him, he used them to feel his way through the gloom. The floor was uneven with many dips and littered with loose chunks of rock that got kicked aside by his hurrying feet. He counted it as more luck that he reached daylight without tripping over.

Behind him, down the shaft, he heard Phelps swearing loudly, blasphemously and crudely.

Emerging on the steep granite slope, Joshua was

dazzled by the brightness of the blazing sun. He hunted cover fast, dodging between the jumbled boulders, heading for yet wilder heights and a notch between two converging ridges.

The shouts of pursuit carried to him.

'He went thataway!' Vince shouted. 'Spread out – surround him – make sure he don't get away!'

'We're only three, Vince,' Phelps grumbled. 'An' I ain't even heeled!'

Through the notch, Joshua found himself in a labyrinth of broken rock – cliffs, walls, crumbling upthrusts and deep ravines. It was time to double-back before he cut off himself off from any route back to his Slash C horse and safety.

Maybe it was also time to turn stalker himself. Scrambling, sliding his way downslope, he found himself overlooking a flat, level area where Vince Waller's second gunnie, a cocked carbine in his hands, was sneaking along, crouching, peering in all directions except up.

If I were Brer Rabbit of the old plantation folk-tales, I'd lie low, Joshua thought. But when going up against murderers and women-takers, that had never been his way.

He shoved his Peacemaker firmly under his belt and, as the man came across the basin and passed directly below, he launched himself at him in a daring dive.

The fellow was borne to the ground, cushioning Joshua's landing, the wind knocked out of him. The carbine escaped his clutches, clattered, bounced on the hard rock and went off shatteringly.

They rolled in the dust and Joshua seized him by the throat.

'Emily Greatheart!' he clipped over the fading echoes of the shot. 'Where've they got her, you sonofabitch? She in the mine?'

The man's eyes boggled – and shifted.

'*Shoot him, Vince! Kill the bastard!*'

Joshua twisted round. At the top of the high, sheer cliff overlooking the basin from the other side, the cold-blooded Waller kid was silhouetted against the vivid blue of the sky. Vince had heard the carbine shot, come at the double – and was this moment aligning the sights of an eight-inch revolver on a target that was Joshua himself!

Joshua flung himself aside and clawed the long-barrelled Peacemaker from his belt in a single flow of movement. The gun kicked twice in his hand an instant before his shoulder hit the ground.

Ninety feet up, Vince's gun-arm was shattered at the elbow and the weapon, a Smith & Wesson Russian .44, span from his nerveless grip, crashing harmlessly with a flash of red from the blue steel muzzle.

The roar of the revolvers merged into one great ear-splitting blast that rang through the basin.

Vince stared in stupid surprise at his bloodied, useless arm. Then he went white and his legs appeared to buckle. He toppled forward slowly off his high perch. For a moment it looked like he would plunge headlong to the rocks below. But halfway down, his fall was arrested by a scrub oak that sprouted tenaciously from a crack in the rock face.

The loop of leather strap by which Vince's field-glasses were strung around his neck snagged a hardy limb of the oak. Vince's feet overtook his checked head and he was brought up with a jerk. Then he twirled. The strap twisted together, became a noose and Vince was abruptly swinging by the neck, choking.

His face went from white to red as it congested with blood. For several seconds, ghastly sounds emerged from his open mouth and he clawed at his constricted throat with his one good hand. His legs scissored in a grotesque dance – an ungraceful pirouette. Then his head adopted an odd, impossible angle on his stretched neck, a bloated tongue protruded from his mouth and he was suspended limply.

'God, mister, he's hung hisself!' the gunnie blurted.

Joshua, though hardened to violent death, was staggered by the turn of events. The chance success of his shot, the chance of the field-glasses' strap hooking the tree branch. . . .

He'd witnessed maybe a hundred ways to die, and knew each man eventually had to find his own. But there was no dignity whatsoever in strangling at the end of string, eyes bulging, tongue forced out and your feet kicking. That was demeaning and horrific.

Despite Vince's big talk, fixing Joshua Dillard had indeed turned out for him to be a pig of a very different bristle from anything he'd envisaged.

Behind Joshua, the Waller gunslick, regaining his amazed wits, thought he saw the opportunity to save his own skin and appease Vince's father, who was going to be mad as a boiled owl. He pounced for his carbine.

Joshua whirled. It was kill or be killed, and the Peacemaker in his fist crashed again.

The carbine toter was flung off his feet. He hauled himself on to his knees, but the bullet had gone close to his heart. Blood was spilling from his body. He expended the last of his will power in an effort to rise to his feet, but the life force was fading out. He collapsed forward full length, face and stomach in the dust, scrabbling with hands and feet till the stillness of death claimed him.

'Poor crazy fool,' Joshua said, his face bleak. 'Couldn't you wait to join your boss in hell?'

More acrid gunsmoke wafted lazily on the hot air, filling the basin with the reek of death. Warily, Joshua scanned the basin's surrounds.

One Waller man, Jake Phelps, was still on the prowl out there, but unarmed. Joshua's guess was that once he was acquainted with the ghastly upshot of the shooting, he'd go back to his calico in the clearing where the grave was sited. Depending on his foolhardiness, he'd return to the hunt with his saddle gun – odds even, one to one – or he'd ride out for the Rocking W.

Tense moments passed and were ended by the clatter of hoofs from nearby as Phelps chose what was probably his wisest option.

Joshua's whole body was aching to the bones with weariness, and his face was bruised and lacerated. He was sure he had two black eyes – the lids were swelling up. A throbbing egg was on the side of his head. But he made himself return to the mine, calling on reserves of endurance while fearing simultaneously he wouldn't find them inexhaustible.

Equipped with one of the lamps, he conducted a thorough search of the deserted workings. He found no underground chamber where a prisoner was or might have been kept. The cavern and tunnels, musty and in places damp, had the desolate air of long abandonment. Nor was there any suggestion to Joshua's mind of unexploited riches at close hand. Frank Clamorgan had been chasing a will-o'-the-wisp.

What his investigation uncovered that was new was a large hole that went down vertically to a lower level. Two ladders were attached to the side of the shaft. One was like the discarded picks and shovels – very old and rotting – but the other was of fresh timber, still white and un-aged. Frank's work? Or some other's?

The promise this dangled before him was short-lived.

Joshua descended by the new ladder. The bottom of the deep pit was unrewarding. It held no sign of habitation. Here, the darkness was extreme and claustrophobic and the walls green and slimy.

Satisfied Emily Greatheart was nowhere in the place, Joshua returned to the barren surface.

The blast of the day's heat was thankfully abating. The sun, a red ball, was dipping toward the jagged purple line of the western horizon and the sky was streaked with crimson and gold. Another day done, and Emily not found.

A new worrying thought bothered Joshua. If Emily had been snatched by Vince Waller, who else knew of her whereabouts now he was dead?

And if she was alive, could she be in worse danger, awaiting food and drink from a jailer who would never be able to return or reveal her well-hidden place of incarceration?

Emily Greatheart lay on her iron-framed bunk and suffered. Her cell was furnished with only the bunk and, set down on the packed dirt floor, a cracked crockery pitcher and bowl, and beside them a leaky slop pail that took the place of a privy in the absence of any more decorous vessel.

The conditions were abominable.

She stretched out on her back, staring up at the ceiling and trying to remember the pleasantnesses of life before she'd come to Arizona. But it was becoming increasingly hard to believe that any other life had ever existed for her; that she'd had a loved and respected father in Denver, a home, a job, a civilized life where decent women were valued and afforded proper protection from the sordid appetites of venal men.

She wondered how long it would be before the man would come – bragging of the rich herds of Slash C cattle he was spiriting away to Mexico to line his pockets . . . and telling her it was time to take his pleasure, make her scream yet again: 'It is what all women are for.'

He'd also suggested to her that he had *amigo*s in

the trade with the cattle and, if after he'd had his fill of her he could arrange it, she might be used by them for a while – passed between them, turn and turn about for their shared amusement. 'As is their way with a young and desirable female captive.'

Emily didn't know if she could survive such brutal and debasing treatment. 'How can you speak of such vile things?' she'd quavered.

He'd leered at her horror. 'It is nothing. Do you want to be made a saint – without flesh and blood and sex? We know that is ridiculous. You are a woman made to be shared *entre camaradas* like an opened bottle of good wine. . . . There is no difference. When we have finished the bottle, we will throw it aside and get another!'

In Denver, she'd occasionally seen the brightly dressed 'sporting girls', plying their trade on Market Street in exchange for money and trinkets. She'd never understood how they could accept their lot as though it were all plain, honest fun. Maybe in time the more fortunate of the unfortunates learned to draw some gratification from the use of their bodies, but what of injury and disease? Indeed, it was reported scarcely a week went by in Denver without two or three swallowing poison.

These were fates Emily had never expected to have to consider on a personal level, and she was very afraid for the future. In the polite world she'd inhabited with her father, with its pruderies and hypocrisies, it was the norm that stigma attached itself to the woman who'd been involved in illicit relations, even if she was forced. Such a woman was regarded as 'fallen' regardless of complicity or its lack.

Emily had mental and bodily hurt from the indignities she'd already undergone, but at a given moment, when she was not under physical invasion, it seemed like something that had happened to somebody else.

With hopes of rescue from her harrowing ordeal sinking every passing hour, she waited in trepidation for the next opening of the iron door . . . and what it might bring.

9

THE BAY HORSE

Joshua Dillard was presented with a new setback when he returned to the arroyo containing the alleged rustler's grave. The borrowed Slash C horse was gone.

He cursed. It had to be Jake Phelps's doing. Leaving him with the arduous trek back to Pike's Crossing was an act of spite, petty revenge for a deserved whupping.

In the oncoming dusk, he felt cold and hugely weary, but he wasn't beaten. Too much time had been lost already in the hunt for Emily Greatheart. He didn't aim to waste more. There should be somewhere in the offing the three mounts ridden to the mine by Vince Waller and his two other sidekicks. None of their owners would be riding them out.

Abruptly Joshua swung away from the arroyo and climbed back up to the mine, where he spent another half-hour casting about fruitlessly among the jumbled boulders and through the prickly patches of twisted, weather-ravaged vegetation.

No sign of the horses was to be found.

Joshua remembered the clatter of hoofs that had reached his ears ending the tense moments after the gunfire in the basin. On reflection, he realized that the amount of noise he'd heard must have been made by more than one horse. Jake Phelps had led out a whole string, probably reined together.

A bitter fury rose in his dry throat that ripe cussing did nothing to abate.

Recognizing the futility of expending his drained reserves of energy on his anger, Joshua started walking away from the scrub-matted, broken hills, back to the grassland of Welcome Valley and the road that cut across it to the Pike's Crossing township.

His walk was soon more of a stumble, but he kept going, putting one foot ahead of the other in determined haste. He kept a close watch for trouble through slitted eyes, and his hand was never far from his gun butt.

Interrupted in his supper at the Rocking W, Bart Waller flung down a fork, tore off a napkin and strode from the big main parlour to his office, where Jake Phelps was asking to see him.

He'd already waited the meal for his son without result and was in a foul temper.

'Well, what is it?' he rapped. 'Is it about Vince?'

'I'll say it is!' Phelps burst out, anxious to deliver a suitable account of Vince Waller's demise and to exonerate himself. 'Vince is dead. It was that crooked range dick Joshua Dillard – attacked us like a crazy 'Pache – beat me within an inch o' my life – strung up Vince from a tree—'

Waller's face clouded. His expression passed in an instant from blank incredulity to fiery, murderous passion. He threw himself at the rat-faced top hand and gripped him savagely by the throat.

'Vince hanged! Is this true, blast you?' he raged. 'Is it a fact?' Big though Phelps was, he was of similar size and shook him like a rag-doll.

Phelps choked. He clawed at Waller's hands. 'Yuh bet it's fac's!' he managed to push out through clenched teeth. 'Ev'ry last damn word of it. . . . *M'throat!*'

Waller let go of him and moved to a roll-top desk. Leaning on it, he pulled out a bottle of whiskey.

'Hell, man, I need a stiff drink!'

He remained in a white-hot frenzy, a bull at a gate. His eyes were feverishly bright as he tipped liquor into a glass, a series of clinks betraying shaking hands. He gulped down two six-ounce glasses of fiery spirit in quick succession.

Phelps rubbed his throat, marked with the imprint of Waller's strong fingers. 'Reck'n I could use one m'self, Bart.'

Waller corked the bottle and threw it at him.

'Help yourself, but be quick about it. I want the story again, slow and full – right from the beginning. . . . Then this must be taken care of, y'unnerstand?'

'But good, Bart.'

Waller nodded, now raring to go. 'The most

important thing comes first, and you know what that is. We saddle up and go get my son's body.'

His lips twisted. 'After that, we root out the boy's saddlebum killer and replant him in Boot Hill!'

Joshua Dillard limped into Pike's Crossing. He chose not to go straight to the Grand Hotel and his bed, which was a tempting possibility. He could imagine the stir it might cause, crossing the lobby in his present state, his face beaten and his clothes torn and filthy. He felt like he'd walked around the world in eighty minutes.

He took himself to Doctor McAdams's house – '*Homage to the Lord*' – and jangled the bell in the side porch. Joshua wondered about the sign. He was beginning to see the tie-up in the conduct of a medico who'd spouted Scripture at him on his first day in Pike's Crossing and who was over-protective to a patient with a religious obsession and a shrine to a dcad son.

He laughed to himself in a bitter way. Two of Welcome Valley's privileged sons were dead now. That should mark a new chapter in the Clamorgan-Waller feud, even if it brought him no closer to knowing what had happened to Emily Greatheart.

Was he made a mite delirious by his bashing and his long walk?

A light went on inside the hallway beyond the glazed porch door, a shadow approached and bolts were drawn.

'Who is it?' the doctor himself called out. 'What do you want?'

'Dillard! Medical attention. Answers. . . .'

McAdams was shocked when he saw Joshua. 'Good Lord, you're in a fearful state! What happened?'

'Homage to Him,' Joshua quipped, light-headed. 'The Lord, I mean. I'm blessed in that all I need is cleaning up some. Like they say, you should've seen the other feller. *Fellers*, that is. Let me be the first to tell you – Vincent Waller has gotten his neck stretched.'

McAdams blinked. 'Vincent Waller hung?'

'That's what I said. Deader'n a door-nail.'

The saturnine doctor insisted on a fuller account as he mopped at Joshua's wounds and applied iodine in his gloomy, panelled surgery. He also grew increasingly agitated as he took a fuller grasp of the implications.

'You're a double-damned fool, Dillard! Bart Waller will raise Cain as a result of this. Lives will be at stake. Yours and any persons who care to offer you sanctuary. You must quit Pike's Crossing immediately.'

Joshua's mouth took on a flint-hard, determined set. 'That isn't my way, Doc. The Waller kid's death was accident. I shot only to disarm him. I figure I haven't finished what I came here to do. And it's being made not a jot easier by the Waller outfit, by you or by your patient, Mrs Clamorgan.'

McAdams glared at him. He picked up a clean swab and instead of using it on Joshua mopped his own brow. Joshua noted absently that he had thick, stubby fingers for a doctor.

'I don't think you should make such accusations, Dillard,' he said. 'To boot, the situation with Waller

95

and his gang will be ugly.'

Joshua shook his head. 'Vince ain't much to mourn over. He was a louse, I figure – most likely a hundred times over. He was the killer of Frank Clamorgan, not that Frank was a sight better. You know that. These sons of the local rich were a bad lot.'

McAdams's jaw tightened and the spade beard jutted. 'I must ask you to leave my house forthwith.'

'Pronto,' Joshua said, rising to his feet. The welcome here was turning colder by the minute. 'I'm feeling better already for the application of your professional skills, but I can't say your attitudes please me one bit. There's no sense, justice or honour in 'em.'

'Please don't mistake my meaning, Dillard!' McAdams cried after him. 'Haul out of this country for good. Bart Waller is a bad man to buck!'

Joshua left in dudgeon. So I'm a double-damned fool, am I, he thought. Well, you're a useless-damned old one!

Come morning, he meant to probe some more into the affairs of the unhelpful doctor and his relationship with the weird Augusta Clamorgan, though top of his agenda would be a stepping-up of the pressure on the Waller riff-raff.

He had no reason to be thrown into a scare by any of Bart Waller's bully-boy behaviour – or influence in this country – and he wasn't yet convinced the Rocking W hardcases couldn't tell him more about Emily Greatheart's disappearance. At a guess, they or their boss's suddenly departed son had something to do with the mystery despite their unconvincing protestations of ignorance.

With the medico's advice ringing in his ears, Joshua debated inwardly whether he should call on Sheriff Horace Sherman to report the untoward incidents in his bailiwick, starting with the ambush from the mesquite clump.

A wicked game was being played out in Welcome Valley. He sensed the death of Vince Waller was going to prove an unfortunate distraction from his mission in behalf of Big Jack Greatheart. Where had Vince figured in Emily's disappearance?

What gnawed at him most was: if Emily still lived, would the reputedly womanizing hellion's sudden demise prove fatal?

Joshua wished mightily he could have wrung some truth from Vince and his trash, but the odds had been of an order that he'd been lucky to survive the trap laid for him at the mine. It stuck in his craw that none of the yellow-gutted gunslicks had found sand enough in theirs to help a girl in trouble.

He decided reports to the provenly ineffective county law office could wait and set his weary feet in the direction of the Golden Horse saloon. His intention was to buy a medicinal bottle for his aches and take it with him to his hotel room where he could mull over all he'd encountered; the little he'd achieved in a tumultuous first day on the case.

But what he saw tied at the hitch-rail outside the saloon brought him up short.

The bay horse had to be the one that had been ridden by the fleeing bushwhacker who'd tried to kill him on his way with Doc McAdams to the Slash C. Either that or its double.

Joshua approached alertly, jolted out of his tiredness by the unexpected discovery. The saddle on the bay was showy in the Mexican style, a working *vaquero* rig but elaborately stamped and with silver conchos and other decorative touches.

Next, he saw that the horse had a Slash C brand on the left hip.

He ran a gentle hand along the horse's shoulder and lifted the nearside foreleg. The spilling radiance of the saloon's lanterns was adequate to show him the hoof carried a giveaway worn shoe. In Joshua's opinion it was a ninety-five per cent certainty the mount was the bushwhacker's.

The sum of these sudden revelations made him puzzled and thoughtful. He'd had some emergent theories, but the holes and flaws in them were suddenly blown country-miles wider.

He entered the saloon, making his walk a casual saunter as he pushed through the batwings. In fact, his eyes under the bruised and puffy lids were probing sharply.

The place was moderately busy, but he recognized no one. Nor did any patron pay an interest to his arrival, let alone show hostility.

Joshua nodded to the aproned man sitting on a stool behind the counter.

The barkeeper rose, a gross man with a flabby, heavily jowled face and a bored manner. He lumbered toward Joshua.

'What'll it be, stranger?'

He had rank breath and sweat stains on his collarless shirt around the armpits.

'Whiskey. No forty-rod lightning ... that Old Crow, in the bottle,' Joshua answered. He then jerked a thumb over his shoulder. 'Mare out there, big bay. D'you know who's she is?'

'Sure, mister, but I don't expect she'd be fer no sale. That's Ramon Rubriz's cayuse. A fine piece of hossflesh. Rubriz'd be the Slash C range boss an' helps hisself to nothin' but the best. A rising *hombre* in these parts.'

Joshua poured and downed a glass of amber liquor that gave an illusion of revitalization.

'Obliged to you for that,' he said agreeably. 'Now, where is Señor Rubriz?'

'He's upstairs, friend. I don't think he'll want to see yuh. Like I said, his hoss ain't fer sale.'

'He with a woman?'

'Naw. It's jest cards here. This burg, yuh lookin' for a poke, the doves are over to Mattie's.'

'The madam with the boarding house on the cross street.'

The apron chuckled dirtily. 'Yuh got it. 'Sides, Rubriz has more'n he c'n handle. His hot greaser wife on the Slash C is jest the half of it. He's got hisself a new honeypot stashed away someplace secret.'

He turned away to reposition the bottles on the shelves in front of the back-bar mirror from where he'd removed the Old Crow.

Joshua lunged forward, seizing the man's arm in an iron grip. 'What did you say?'

Fear flicked across the barkeep's muddy eyes, for Joshua was intense and his roughed-up appearance didn't inspire confidence that he was a peaceful man. He'd lately been mixed up in a brawl someplace, then incompletely patched up.

'N-nothin', mister – jest as how Rubriz was braggin' to some Mex pals he'd got a fancy woman some place, the sweetest, whitest piece of young ass a man—'

But Joshua had left the bar and was bounding up the stairs two at a time.

'Hey, hold your hosses!' the barkeep yelled after him. 'The card rooms are hired out private – an' who's paying fer this bottle?'

10

RUBRIZ PLAYS HIS CARD

Joshua wondered whether the card room where'd he'd find Ramon Rubriz was the same one where Emily Greatheart's fiancé had met his death.

He barrelled into the first room he came to, flinging back the door, with drawn Peacemaker tight in his fist and cocked. He got lucky. Four men were seated at the playing table in the room, which was heavy with the mingled fumes of tobacco smoke and liquor. One of them was the Slash C range *mayordomo*, Ramon Rubriz.

'Drop the cards and get out!' Joshua ordered. 'Every mother's son, except you, Rubriz. You're staying!'

The three others, rag-tag *peón* types, slunk out. When confronted by a madman armed with a big revolver, discretion over-ruled most any other policy, but Joshua's relieved thought was that they 'scared easy'.

Ash dropped from the end of the brownie stuck habitually to Rubriz's thick lower lip.

'Señor Dillard, what does this mean? Why do you come here like this? Rudely – and mussed up . . . beaten up?'

'Don't play the innocent with me, skunk!' Joshua rapped, kicking the door shut behind the card-players. 'It's time you did some serious talking, and if I don't get straight answers fast I'm going to beat them out of you!'

'This is ridiculous!' Rubriz blustered. 'What is it you want to know?'

'You'll start by admitting and explaining why you tried to drygulch me this morning.'

'I did no such—'

Rubriz broke off with a cry of pain as Joshua raked his face with the Peacemaker's sight. The time was long over for kid-glove methods.

'Try again!'

'All right! All right. . . .' Rubriz cursed. '*Señor*, I acted only to scare you away from the Slash C. You must understand, I am an *hombre* more sinned against than sinning.'

'Sure,' Joshua scoffed. 'Innocent, without blemish! You want I should really cut open your face?'

'But it is truth! For long years, I slave to build up the Slash C herds, devote my life, fight off the Waller wolves, but then Old John Clamorgan dies, and I must work for his stupid wife and spoiled son.'

Joshua listened stonily as the words and the cigarette tumbled from Rubriz's mouth and he unburdened himself.

'Far worse, the opportunist Doctor McAdams means he should marry Augusta and for all the Slash C's wealth – the reward of *my* long work – to pass into his soft and greedy hands. This, I and my Francisca cannot bear. I take Slash C beeves to sell to *amigos* from Old Mexico, to provide for my doubtful future. It is why I shoot at you, *señor* – to scare you away, lest you should unmask and oppose me in the just striving for what is fair and mine.'

'My heart bleeds for you,' Joshua said sarcastically. 'Rustling your own outfit's stock! But I don't take any scare, and your infamy doesn't end there, does it? You're a foul lecher also, and you've helped yourself to Frank Clamorgan's girl – Emily Greatheart!'

Rubriz spread his hands in weak protest. 'I know nothing of the girl, *señor*. Why should I interfere with her? All women are alike in the dark . . . is this not so?' He smirked. 'At Mattie's I buy any *puta* I like for a few dollars.'

'Damn you, Rubriz – you lie in your rotten brown teeth! The apron downstairs heard you bragging to your pards like Pecos Bill!'

Rubriz either panicked or found a hidden reserve of foolish courage. Unexpectedly uncoiling his sinewy form, he brought the round poker table up with knees and hands. The board rose, scattering coin, paper, chips and pasteboard, and behind its cover he tilted his Colt in the holster and fired through the slit-bottomed leather.

The smash of two guns merged in a single roar.

The hanging lamp rattled and layers of tobacco smoke briefly parted as the slugs whistled to their marks.

Rubriz's shot nicked cloth from Joshua's right sleeve, near the shoulder. Joshua's shot parted Rubriz's lank hair, flinging him to the floor but leaving him sufficiently conscious to thumb back the hammer of his .45 and bring it into line for a second attempt to eliminate his persecutor.

'*Muerte a gringos!*' he snarled.

Joshua paused only for the instant it took the recoil of his Peacemaker to settle, then he fired again. His aim was precise; the squeeze of his trigger finger steady. Even so, Rubriz was moving and the lead thumped into his gut instead of merely disarming him. At this close range, a Colt .45 slug tore a hole in a man too big to survive. Gunplay, Joshua noted, not for the first time in his career, was no exact science.

Rubriz allowed his gun to fall and, clutching his belly with both hands, watched the blood pulse from the fatal wound through his fingers. He was defiant to the last; proud of his despicable crime to his miserable end.

'*Hijo de puta!*' he spat at Joshua. 'You will never find the woman now! And *sí*, she was good – untouched and exciting – and in the hiding-place where her cries are never heard, I took her like no other man ever had . . . or c-can!'

He faltered, his face gone bloodless and screwed up in pain. 'It is not – in the cards – for me to live – range dick. *But I have won!*'

With a final heaving groan, Ramon Rubriz gave up his tenuous hold on life.

Simultaneously, the door to the card room was flung open. The heads of Pike's Crossing citizens were poked around both jambs. Concerned, apprehensive, they were anxious to know the cause and results of the shooting upstairs.

Joshua swung his gun to cover the opening.

'Far enough, gents! Only person needed in here is the undertaker.'

Joshua was angry it had proved necessary for his approach to Rubriz to end in gunfire, still more that the man had died without revealing where Emily Greatheart was hidden. On the credit side, he knew now she was still alive, though in what condition he dared not guess. Nor could he guess how long she'd stay alive if her abductor was dead.

Also to advantage, Joshua had it confirmed Denholm McAdams was deep into an agenda of his own. The pieces of certain puzzles fell into place. He suspected it had been the doctor who'd tipped off Rubriz about his impending visit to the Slash C, allowing the range boss to stage his ambush from the mesquite. He remembered how McAdams had let his buggy crash from the roadway, thus setting him up for Rubriz to make further attempts to kill him.

Joshua's next port of call had to be to the medico's office. He promised himself the return visit would be no gentle affair. If McAdams had been in cahoots with Rubriz for the bushwhacking, it meant he (the doc) hadn't wanted him probing around at the Slash C either. With Rubriz dead, Joshua aimed to get the answers someplace about what really went on in the Clamorgan camp.

In the passage and down the stairs, a cry was going up: 'Get Sheriff Sherman!'

Joshua crossed to the window and drew back the dirty striped curtain to peer out. The slovenly barkeep was already scurrying toward the law office, apron flapping in the night breeze.

He swore. A night in a cold and hard jail cell, pressed with questions for which he couldn't supply answers – asked to explain not one but four violent deaths when you counted the Wallers' toll – had no part in Joshua's plans.

No sooner was he confronted with this distinctly unwelcome possibility than came a new, equally disturbing development. From the far end of the main street, where the roadway curved out of town and across the bridge over the wide creek, came the drumbeat rumble of many hoofs.

Bart Waller surged into town at the head of a bunch of tough Rocking W riders. They reined in outside the Grand Hotel in a great cloud of dust that floated in the lamps' light like a yellow fog. With strident, shrill whoops, they blazed guns off into the air. But these were no rollicking cowpokes on a Saturday-night spree. They were killers come to do murder.

Joshua went to Rubriz's slack body and removed his well-filled cartridge belt. He buckled it round his own lean hips. The affair was coming to a boil faster than a red-hot kettle, and under such circumstances a man like himself needed ammunition – the plentier, the safer.

Back at the window, he watched Waller's crew bring their milling, prancing horses to a standstill. Their big boss was raising his hands for the commotion to cease.

Facing the hotel, Bart Waller bellowed, 'Dillard! Joshua Dillard! I want you! Come on out!'

Sheriff Horace Sherman bustled along from his office, toting a shotgun, frowning heavily.

'What is this, Waller? Yuh've gotten folks plumb scairt outa their wits with all the damn' hollerin' and shootin'!'

Waller eyed him balefully. 'The gunfighter Dillard has killed my boy – hanged him! He's gotta die. Eye for an eye, tooth for a tooth!'

'Vince dead. . . ?'

'You heard me right, tin-badge!'

Sherman, to his credit, digested the startling news fast. 'Waal, be that as mebbe, but under law in this town, thar's due process afore a man goes to the gallows. Lay your complaint an' this Dillard'll be arrested.'

Waller put a splattering globule of saliva into the dust at Sherman's feet.

'I despise you, I despise your two-bit town, Sherman! Lemme get at Dillard, or my boys shoot the place to bits, burn it down around your goddamned ears!'

The Golden Horse barkeep bobbed forward out the shadows of a shop awning where he'd sheltered fearfully from the gun-firing gang.

'Ain't no call fer that, Mister Waller, sir! He's over

to the saloon. Just done shot a – a party!'

The barkeep knew his local politics and that a Slash C death would cut no particular ice with the ruler of the rival Rocking W empire.

Joshua cursed. He was trapped again, outnumbered and in deadly danger. The chances he could turn the tables as he had at the old Spanish mine were incredibly slim. The noose of a hangrope loomed dangerously close. For while a court of law might be swayed to absolve him of guilt in connection with the death of Vince Waller, in the eyes of the citizens of Pike's Crossing he would be standing between them and escape from fiery destruction.

When it came to the choice, he knew they'd hand him over to Vince's vengeance-mad father. Nor did surrendering himself to Sherman seem like a practical course. How would the sheriff hold off the gang of well-paid, hardened owlhoots Waller had in lieu of honest men working for straight cow-hands' wages?

And if incarceration in a cell in the sheriff's jailhouse did offer a slim measure of protection, equally it would prevent him from pursuing the doubly urgent hunt for Emily Greatheart.

Joshua flung up the sash as far as it would go. 'I'm up here, Waller!'

The big cattleman twisted in the saddle and looked up.

'You bastard, Dillard!' he snarled savagely, his face congested darkly with hate. 'You've pushed the last of your luck. I'm gonna see you down here and dead!'

'Listen! Hear me good, Waller. Seems you're in

the dark about certain things. Get it clear I didn't kill your son. That's Jake Phelps's lie! Vince fell. The hanging was accident. The leather strap on his field-glasses broke his neck. Didn't you go see for yourself? What did you find?'

Waller hesitated, kneading his reins in a ham-like fist. 'Hell!' he snorted finally, anger still edging his voice. 'You think I come here to play coroner?'

'An ambitious man like yourself should've learned someplace how to tell the difference between truth and lies, Waller,' Joshua said calmly, picking his words carefully, knowing he was walking a fine line between cooling passions and inflaming them. 'Did what you found say I strung Vince up?'

Phelps shoved his horse forward, coming between his boss and Joshua, cutting off Joshua's appeal to sanity. He fixed Joshua with his glittering rat's eyes, the light in them red by some trick of reflected lamp-light. Plainly the last thing he wanted was for Bart Waller to consider what Joshua had said, to put it under the light of unemotional reason. Expose him as a liar.

'Mebbe so yuh've said too much yuhself already, killer range dick!'

Joshua saw a small chance he could stop the whole business unravelling in an orgy of lead-slinging, multiple deaths and maybe the firing of a whole town.

'You reckon the time for talking's over, is that it, Jake Phelps?'

'Sure! Same as your killin' days are over!'

Joshua prodded some more, slyly. 'You offering to

accommodate me – that the deal, Phelps? No words. A shootout, man to man?'

Phelps got it now. Joshua Dillard had tricked him into making a challenge of his bid to shut him up over the truth about Vince's death. He couldn't lose face with a whole hushed and expectant town looking on.

He swallowed the sour taste of the trick. He was a rat, but no cornered rat. Given even chances, he was good with a gun.

'Yeah, Dillard! Come on down from thar. I'm waitin'!'

11

SHOOTOUT ON MAIN STREET

Sleep wouldn't come to Francisca Rubriz. Long into the night, she awaited the return of her husband, determined to have out with him the matter that was tearing their shaky marriage apart.

Whether she'd let him actually return to their bed, where his half remained cold and empty, was beyond immediate resolution. It would depend, she decided, on Ramon's total and abject contrition for what he had done to her. He had broken their vows, insulted her profoundly. The teasing taunts he'd always made about the faint shadow of dark hair over her upper lip, blighting connubial bliss from the start, paled into insignificance against the deed he'd boasted of.

Twisting the thick gold wedding band on her finger, she rose out of the loveless bed. The room – allotted to the *mayordomo* in the Clamorgan *hacienda*

111

itself – was spacious but sparsely furnished. The bed, with dark, hardwood posts, dominated; a dresser matched. But a cheval mirror framed in paler wood didn't seem entirely to belong.

Francisca stood before the mirror.

Moonlight shafted through the tall windows and bounced off whitewashed walls, silhouetting her ample shape. She smoothed both hands over ample hips, moulding the flimsy nightgown to her lush body. She spat an epithet, pursing her lips so her face was more than ever like a fat, riled cat's. She thrust herself forward aggressively at the mirror. Was she not abundantly female?

There was woman enough between her hands for any man, she answered herself. Ramon should have been satisfied in performance of his duty to her. The heat of anger warmed her in the coolness of the room.

She shucked the revealing nightgown and concealed her thick, spouse-neglected body in a long black dress, fastening the two dozen buttons down the front with strong but deft fingers. She lit a lamp, turned it low, and left the room, taking a long white-washed corridor paved with age-worn handmade tiles, heading for the kitchen which was her daytime domain.

She busied herself, hefting wood for the cook-stove. Here, too, the floor was tile and the domed and raftered ceiling high and echoing.

The noise she made brought Augusta Clamorgan herself to investigate, a shawl draped from her gaunt shoulders over her night attire.

'Francisca! It must be almost midnight. What are you doing?'

Francisca was not at all dismayed by her employer's arrival and the peevish inquiry. A show-down was what she wanted. Nothing had ever been quite right here since the death of *el patrón*, old John Clamorgan.

Young Frank Clamorgan – who'd habitually spied on her when she'd been in her bathtub but never been chastised or so much as reprimanded by his doting mother – had been no loss. And the delicate, lily-skinned charms of his fiancée from Denver were the cause of her latest and most serious troubles. They'd taken Ramon from her.

She faced up to the tall, haggard widow.

'You are not the only woman with her losses, *señora*,' she said acidly. 'Who is given sleepless nights meditating on the wickedness of the she-devil you have made the unwilling guest of this household?'

Augusta Clamorgan peered more closely at her. 'You are upset, Francisca Rubriz, and have no right to speak to me in such a disrespectful tone. Through the girl of whom you speak, I have lost my *son*.'

'And I have lost my husband!'

'Ramon. . . ?' Augusta said. 'I don't understand. He is dead?'

Francisca worked herself up into a fever-pitch of anger, the woman scorned. 'No! The dog has had his way with *her* – she who you keep here to purify so that she is fit to join your precious boy when she becomes his bride in Heaven!'

'There's much we have to teach Emily Greatheart

so that she is properly angelic, but—'

'No buts!' Francisca's lip curled in mockery. 'The innocent Señorita Emily is *Señora Satán* herself. She has sinned against God. She has excited the stallion streak in my Ramon with her devious city wantonness. It is the consequence of your loco schemes!'

Still barely comprehending, Augusta demanded, 'Where is Ramon?'

'Ridden to town to escape my wrath and celebrate his filthy adultery. There he will stiffen himself with liquor, reviving his drained vigour so he can fornicate with your high-toned miss again!'

The manic light in Augusta Clamorgan's eyes blazed. For a terrible moment her lined face was a mask of ancient evil. Her frame quivered with tension. Then slowly she relaxed, and even the wrinkles seemed less deeply etched. She laughed throatily.

She groped in a kitchen drawer and produced a sharply edged skinning knife that narrowed to a curved point. It coruscated in the lamplight, and she turned it delicately in gnarled but powerful fingers.

Francisca's blood ran cold.

Augusta said, 'The unfaithful hussy! She will have to be transfigured. It will put her beyond Ramon's pleasure . . . and render her fit in the hereafter for my darling Frank!'

'Come on down, Dillard!' Jake Phelps yelled again. 'We'll clear the street an' I'll be waiting fer yuh in the middle, down the road apiece, alongside that big cottonwood . . . to see if yuh wanna shoot it out or git strung up!'

Bart Waller put in, 'I give you no more'n ten minutes, saloon bum. You don't show, we'll burn you outa that dump!'

His fingers working automatically, Joshua reloaded his Peacemaker. It didn't take him many minutes. When he'd finished, he wedged the gun tightly into its holster. On feet aching from weariness, he clumped his way down the creaking stairs of the Golden Horse.

In a snug corner, an old-timer Joshua recognized as a man who did odd jobs around the Grand Hotel, took a long gulp from his beer glass and wiped foam from his whiskers.

'Yuh're gonna have to be mighty fast, mister,' he wheezed. 'Jake Phelps is a bad 'un to cross. Johnny Ringo, Wes Hardin and Curly Bill Brocius wasn't a patch on the sonofabitch.'

Joshua nodded acknowledgement of the warning and stumped on. He had no knowing how this desperate gamble was going to work out. If he came through the shootout, would he then be free to force from Denholm McAdams the truth he suspected he knew about Emily Greatheart's captivity? Or would Bart Waller deny him even the roughest of justice that was a gun duel, and persist with his desire to make him pay for his son's stupid death?

The street had miraculously cleared and Jake Phelps was waiting as he'd said he'd be, clear of the darker patch of shadow cast by the cottonwood. It was a gallows tree, its stark limbs etched against the moonlight. Phelps was standing there in a gunfighter's crouch, shoulders hunched, his right hand hovering over the ivory butt of the Colt nestled in a supple-looking, well-worn holster.

He had death in his eyes.

'Come on, asshole!' he grated. 'Make your grab!'

But his voice was tinged with excitement, and Joshua sensed with an exultation born of a half-hundred similar encounters that Phelps wasn't as confident as he professed and was excessively eager to have the clash over and done with.

Joshua knew of old that a fast draw wasn't everything. He figured Jake Phelps was of the breed that hurried so much that they missed with their first shot. That didn't matter when they were intimidating a greenhorn. The poor devil would panic under fire and be dead from the second anyway. But Joshua was a seasoned gunfighter, even though the reputation wasn't of his choosing. His chances were therefore better than the greenhorn's and he made his game plan accordingly.

He kept pacing forward evenly till he was a scant twenty yards from Phelps. Then he let his hand dip toward the blackened grips of the Peacemaker, but didn't complete the draw.

As Phelps whipped his Colt from greased leather, Joshua dived to the ground and did a full forward somersault. He heard the crash of Phelps's shot but felt nothing. The gunslick's first shot had passed over him harmlessly.

Joshua completed his roll upright on his knees. He hauled out the Peacemaker, while simultaneously throwing himself bodily sideways full length in the dust.

The lightning-fast, athletic manoeuvres flummoxed Phelps. It was the first time he'd seen a gunfighter pull such a startling stunt. He let loose with a second shot that proved as wild as the first when the moment had come for the coolest of heads, a steady hand and a precise aim.

From his close-in position on the ground, Joshua raised the cocked Peacemaker on his extended arm and squeezed the trigger. The gun roared, the muzzle flashed redly. The .45 slug made a bloody hole, big as a new mouth, that reduced Phelps's face to an unrecognizable ruin.

He was dead before his heavy body hit to the roadway with a dust-raising whump like an axed tree. His pulped face was hidden in the dirt but the gory mess that was the back of his shattered skull was just as likely to turn the strongest man's stomach, its contents open to the night sky.

Joshua had no time to feel any pity for the man – a liar and a troublemaker who'd reportedly taken pay to assist and protect a powerful cattle baron's randy son in his miserable adventures. Jake Phelps had failed in his job and paid a grim price.

Joshua's sole concern now was to find Emily Greatheart. Vince Waller had proved a false trail where she was concerned. Precious hours had been wasted. Late as it was, tired as he was, what he'd learned from the dying Ramon Rubriz made a further interview with the saturnine Doctor McAdams an imperative. McAdams had deliberately misled him, consistently pointing him in the Wallers' direction and setting him up to take Rubriz's bushwhack bullets.

Did the medico know where Emily was?

Joshua was about to turn away, a little groggily, when he felt the hard pressure of a gun barrel in his back.

Sheriff Horace Sherman said softly, 'I'm takin' your gun, Dillard. Yuh're under arrest fer murder!'

Joshua was astounded. 'What the hell—? It was a fair fight. Jake Phelps called me out.'

'Nope. Not fer Phelps's murder. Nor fer Ramon Rubriz. Fer the murder of Vincent Waller. I've got two deputies with me an' we'll act accordin' to law if'n yuh start fightin'.'

'Vince Waller wasn't murdered, Sheriff. Who's putting that about now?'

'Bart Waller has sworn a statement, a complaint quotin' a witness.'

'Yeah – Jake Phelps, and he's dead!'

'Then it'll be your word ag'inst Bart Waller's. I'll hold yuh, let a judge decide. Yuh got nothin' to fear.'

Joshua swore bitterly. 'You fool! I've got work to do. I've still to find Miss Emily Greatheart, remember?'

'At this time o' night. . . ? Fergit it anyhow! The Greatheart gal's long gone, a closed case. Consider this fer your own continued health, Dillard. Raise your han's!'

'I don't believe this play! Who's suckering who?'

Sheriff Sherman stood back, still menacing Joshua with his gun. One of the armed deputies stepped forward and removed Rubriz's cartridge belt.

Defiantly, Joshua said, 'There'll be hell to pay for

this, Sherman. No court will ever convict me on trumped-up evidence from a distraught father. I'll say plenty, believe me. They'll have your badge!'

'I'm a duly elected sheriff,' Sherman said stiffly. 'The voters'll have last say on that, an' most of 'em do as Wallers or Clamorgans tell 'em.'

Townsfolk were starting to reappear on the street, talking in hushed whispers. A dog barked and rattled a chain noisily inside a fenced yard.

Bart Waller and his men were nowhere in sight – which was odd, Joshua thought. They weren't the type to have been upset by the sight of Phelps's violent end. In any case, their sidekick's death had ranked as a possibility from the outset – one, more-over, which had obviously been partly anticipated. Maybe Waller thought his swift legal moves had him sewn up for now.

It was all somewhat more than a tired brain could process. That Waller might think he could make his charge stick long-term was absurd.

Sherman and his helpers escorted him closely through the town's semi-darkness to the jailhouse.

12

DEATH BY THE ROPE

Bart Waller led his full crew of riders minus Jake Phelps no further than the bridge, where he pulled up, erect in his saddle.

There, above the lap and gurgle of the broad creek, a disgruntled henchman growled, 'Why'd yuh turn him over to the law, boss?'

He was backed by a rumbling chorus of similar disapproval. These were men who followed a code that said business was done differently. Honour didn't sit well with them, fair shootout or no. One sombre fear taking seed was that Waller had suffered some lapse in his mental faculties, a premature senility brought on by the death of his son.

'There's more ways to skin a cat. . . .' Waller said, resting his big hands on the saddle pommel and leaning forward earnestly. 'Vince was cruelly put to death. We got his killer locked in the jailhouse so as we know that's where we find him. I don't want to be galloping all over the landscape.'

A hardcase chuckled. 'Gotta hand it to yuh, Bart, that's smart.'

Another wasn't so sure. 'He goes before any judge, the ol' coot is as apt to slap him on the wrist whiles pattin' him on the back. Jake hadn't no friends on judicial benches.'

'Dillard ain't having a trial,' Waller said impatiently. 'I'm figuring the only judge he'll face is Judge Lynch, and he don't ask for evidence from the accused. Find us a rope. We get the job done tonight.'

None of them could see any flaw in that. They turned their horses back in the direction of the town's lights.

Joshua sensed time was running out. It had been a hard day and it was being followed by a hard night. He was tired to the bone, but instinct told him he couldn't afford to languish in the cell to which Sheriff Sherman was prodding him.

'Welcome to the cleanest jail in the county, Dillard,' Sherman said.

Joshua paused in the doorway to the bar-fronted cell, noting the neat stack of clean blankets on the wooden bunk against the far adobe wall.

'I'd sure enjoy the rest, Sheriff, but it also don't seem wise somehow.'

Sherman jangled the keys. 'Let me put it to yuh diff'rently, Dillard. It ain't wise fer yuh to be anyplace else. I figure Bart Waller is on the prod, buildin' a necktie party fer yuh, savvy? I aim to keep yuh alive!'

Joshua belatedly refined his assessment of the sheriff – he was a thickly muscled, powerful man who had the look of one who would fight for what he believed was right even if he was wrong; even if he sometimes came short on brain power. Joshua had, during his law-enforcement years, mixed with men like him. He'd found out, even when playing his preferred lone hand, that if you were in a tight spot – a fight with fists or guns maybe – the men it was best to have alongside you were built exactly Sherman's way.

It was the time element that bothered Joshua most. Too many valuable hours had been spent tangling with the Wallers and it had brought him nothing but a mess of trouble. Rubriz's death had put him on the edge of a breakthrough; Vince's, once revealed to his pa, had cancelled it out.

Joshua said, 'It's for my own protection, my own good, huh?' Then, giving some shrewd thought to it, he added, 'Well, you set yourself up as the brave, honest sheriff, we'll see how it pans out when Waller and his hounds come howling.'

Sherman's bushy brows lowered. 'Don't get me wrong, Dillard, I ain't no dirty yeller dog. Them hounds'll be in fer a hell of a fight.'

In the event, the promptness of the Waller bunch's audacity was unexpected by Sherman, but welcomed by Joshua, who was fretful of delay and anxious for action – any action that might release him to follow his quest.

Waller cantered back into Pike's Crossing a scant fifteen minutes after he'd left it. A rope hadn't taken his band long to find, despite their shaky *bona fides* as cowpokes.

The aggrieved cattleman hollered his demands outside the jailhouse.

'Sherman! You hand over that dirty saddlebum killer straight away, you hear? He ain't welcome in Welcome Valley an hour longer. He gets his tonight, just like my Vince and Jake Phelps!'

Inside, Sherman grumbled to his two deputies. 'Damned two-legged coyote. Unchain four shotguns from the wall rack an' see they're loaded.'

'Four?' queried one of the law-pups.

'You heard, kid. Four. That's one fer Dillard, too. Comes to shootin', we're outnumbered here awful bad. An extra shotgunner c'd mean your ma won't have to tote flowers to a grave ev'ry Sunday from here on.'

From outside came another bellow. 'Sherman! Answer me, blast you!'

Joshua said, 'God! He's roaring like a bee-stung bear. What chance do I have, cooped up in here?'

Sherman shoved his keys through the bars. 'Yuh c'n let yuh self out, Dillard, but no tricks, mind. Jest as a precaution – case things git out o' hand.'

To Waller, Sherman yelled, 'Vamoose, Waller! Dillard stays in jail till he stands trial. Yuh got no argument with the law, an' in Pike's Crossin' that's me!'

Waller glared at the jailhouse, his underlip thrust forward, studying on it, but not for long.

'You're all washed up in this county, Sheriff,' he barked back, a decision made. 'We're coming on in!'

Waller was wrong on both counts. Sherman was making a stand on his authority, and he was barring the Rocking W gang access. He stepped out on to the front porch clutching a primed ten-gauge, flanked by his deputies, identically armed.

The shotguns were fearsome weapons, but Sherman had underestimated the ruthless gunslicks who were dismounting out front of his office – their loyalty bought, their courage bolstered by the bounty offered them by Bart Waller.

He'd also not recognized the depravity of Waller himself, accentuated beyond reason by the loss of his son, only heir to the empire he'd been building steadily in competition with the hated Clamorgans.

'Don't do nothin' foolish, bravos!' Sherman snapped. 'This ain't worth a bloodba—'

Waller was still mounted. His side-arm blurred out of the holster and was cocked and triggered in one eye-deceiving movement. The Colt crashed and bucked. Sherman was hit in the leg, but his scream as the broken limb dumped him sprawling on the plankwalk was drowned out. The hammers of his own wildly swinging shotgun also fell, producing a great, explosive roar.

The heavy buckshot scythed across man and beast indiscriminately, painting a bloody red arc. Squealing horses toppled, threshing their limbs in death throes. Three of Waller's men died instantly, flung headlong on the roadway.

Their sidekicks began firing at the front of the law

office. Glass smashed; splinters flew. One young deputy dropped his shotgun, which skittered off the walk into the dust unfired, and fled for cover behind a rain barrel. The other shot one barrel of his scattergun to small effect – messily ripping open the belly of a fallen horse – before he, like the sheriff, was cut down to writhe in agony on the boards.

Meanwhile, inside the office, Joshua was throwing down the loaned shotgun and buckling on his confiscated Peacemaker and gunbelt, which he considered an altogether more practical rig for what he had in mind.

Disregarding the horror of what was going down out front, he shoved a rickety desk across the room to a side wall with a high window. He jumped on to the desk and tried to open the window, only to find it jammed. He climbed up on to the sill and perched there in a crouch, hammering out the panes and framing with the butt of his trusty Peacemaker. Glass tinkled, but the betraying sounds were lost in the cacophony of gunfire and smashing panes at the front.

With the last jagged shards removed, Joshua wriggled out feet first to drop into a side alley. He sped to the back of the block and ducked along behind the darkened bank. When he came to the next alley, a mere dogtrot, he went through it to the main street. The roadway here was deserted, cleared of any late roamers by the deadly fracas outside the sheriff's office.

A stroke of luck! Outside the Golden Horse saloon, Ramon Rubriz's big bay mare still stood at the hitch-rail, head drooped, tail swishing, unaware her rider would not be returning. Forgotten.

Joshua didn't need a horse to get him to Doctor McAdams, but he would to outrun Waller and his gang when they found he wasn't in the jailhouse and started tearing the town apart. Moreover, it seemed certain Emily Greatheart was detained someplace on the Slash C, where Rubriz had been able to take advantage of her. He should have figured it all out much, much earlier. But self-recrimination achieved nothing. He'd need a mount to carry him there and free her – before more harm befell her; if she was still alive.

Joshua hastily untied the horse and was leading her away in the direction of the medico's house, when the luck ran out. He was spotted.

'*Yonder he goes, the bastard!*'

The sharp-eyed roughneck, one of the several still milling around Sherman's office, lifted his gun and fired twice.

The shots smashed out.

One bullet missed Joshua's head by a fraction of an inch. He felt the hot wind of it. It thunked into a sign nailed to a post at the livery-barn runway.

The other whistled on up the road, falling spent somewhere near the stage company's corralyard.

'After him, men! Stop him!' Waller screamed, foaming at the mouth.

Joshua fitted his boot into the bay's left stirrup and swung up into the fancy Mexican saddle.

'Giddap, critter!' he cried. He put his heels into the animal's sides and lashed her into rapid movement with the rein ends.

The horse was well-trained and not too docile to produce a good turn of speed at short order. Drifting clouds obscured the moon every other passing moment, but the horse seemed to know the road, which was flanked by an avenue of cottonwoods, and the thin starlight showed Joshua all he needed to see.

Waller and his bunch of riders gave pounding chase, but Joshua reckoned he was their equal as a horseman and his mount the more rested.

He turned in the saddle and with one steadying hand on the cantle, squeezed off two shots from the Peacemaker. He knew his chances of finding a target while at full gallop were next to nil, but the threat of flying lead had a way of deterring pursuers, slowing them down.

A rapid series of dully echoing clops told Joshua he was crossing the bridge over the creek. He turned his eyes ahead. Someplace in the wild, dark distance with a howling, unofficial posse at his heels wasn't where he wanted to be.

As soon as they came off the bridge, Joshua hauled hard on the reins, sliding the mare to a stop. Then he slewed her sharp left, and clucked her down a steep slope to the creek bank. Ducking his head, he tucked himself and the horse out of sight in the black shadows under the bridge.

Waller and his men thundered overhead, almost scaring the life out of the bay mare. He calmed her with a patting hand, a scheme hurriedly shaping up in his mind. Soon as his hunters realized he wasn't ahead, they would come storming back.

He started the mare moving again, returning over the bridge. He went as far as the part of the road that was dappled by the darker shadows of the flanking cottonwoods. Here, on the town's shirt-tail outskirts, he pulled up again.

The bay was rigged for the work of a vaquero, with a strong, horsehair lariat slung from the saddle. Joshua slid to the ground and got to work, fast.

He picked out two trees that were close to the trail on opposite sides. He uncoiled the lariat, ran it round one trunk, tied a knot and darted over the road to the other side where he repeated the exercise with the other trunk. He pulled the rope taut at a level about one foot above the roadway before securing it with a last knot.

'Now the devil take the paid killers!' he muttered coldly. 'They don't rate the mercy I'd give a nest of rattlers.'

He walked the bay under the trees and yanked her into complete concealment behind brush. The horse snorted and tossed her head as dimly visible barbed growth attacked her chest and flanks. Once there, the sweating horse was calm enough despite fresh scratches and the burrs that clung here and there to her coat. She began cropping at the lower tree growth, looking for buds and tender shoots.

The wait was a short one.

The sound of galloping hoofs drumming back over the bridge, accompanied by men's hurled profanities and imprecations, announced the hell-raising band's approach. Bart Waller was in the lead, vowing vengeance with more venom than ever, his apoplectic face flushed livid. He'd been tricked, shown up in front of his owlhoot henchmen.

'He can't-a got fur! His fish is fried, damnit!'

None of the racing riders saw the stretched rope as they came spurring pell-mell down the trail.

In the brush, the bay mare – sweat on neck and around the fancy saddle drying in the cool night air – shivered as though in premonition.

Waller's unfortunate horse hit the rope first and spilled in a heap to the ground with a broken leg. The crash reverberated through the earth under Joshua's feet many yards away. Because of their hectic pace, the following riders were unable to pull up. Screeching horses piled up on the obstacle of the leader, in a domino effect.

Waller had been hurled from the saddle into the air. His heels went over his head and he crashed down almost as heavily as his horse. The top of his skull hit the ground first, and he came to rest like a floppy doll, his limbs and head all at the oddest angles.

Like son, like father, Joshua thought . . . another broken neck.

13

"TELL ME, DOCTOR"

Lamps were still burning behind curtains in Doctor McAdams's house when Joshua rode back briskly into Pike's Crossing. At a guess the medico had had a busy night with calls for his services from the wounded victims of the gunplay at the sheriff's office and jailhouse.

McAdams, he further guessed, wouldn't be expecting to see him again. His involvement in Ramon Rubriz's bushwhacking play was more obvious than ever in the light of reflection and later knowledge. Advised that Joshua had fled town with a bloodlusting Waller and his crowd hot on his scent like a pack of rabid hounds, McAdams would probably be resting a deal easier, thinking his dastardly secrets were safe.

Joshua aimed to keep this advantage till he had the man at his untender mercy.

He hadn't tarried under the cottonwoods to see what the remnants of Waller's gang would do. With noisy disarray at its height, he'd pushed the mare through the brush, patted her neck with a soothing word or two and climbed back to the saddle. He'd rejoined the road closer to town. He didn't think the gunslicks would resume the manhunt, not with their paymaster plainly dead.

He tied the bay behind some two-storey residences in a quiet cross street. Although he'd been in McAdams's house twice, he'd not gone further than a hallway and the medico's surgery. He'd noted he was a bachelor and appeared to have no live-in servants.

Joshua reckoned his appearance alone would likely be enough to throw a scare into the gloomy doctor.

His clothes were filthy, much creased and in places torn. The dark, short-tailed coat was blotched with dust, the grey pants were out at the knee, his shirt was soiled and limp, the string tie had lost its knot, his hand-made Justin boots were badly scuffed.

The catalogue was dispiriting. Restoration of these items alone was going to eat up the larger part of what was left of Big Jack Greatheart's modest advance on account of his expenses.

Many of the bruises and cuts on his swollen and unshaven face McAdams had seen before, but his subsequent exertions had undone the doctor's clean-up work with suitably shocking results. The salt of his sweat stung multiple abrasions.

Joshua passed up the side porch with its inviting bell and the doctor's godfearingly declaratory shingle and went exploring. A night bird cooed plaintively someplace, reminding Joshua of the sounds he'd heard in Augusta Clamorgan's chapel that McAdams had put down to nesting pigeons. A dog began barking across town, and the racket was taken up by others.

Back of the house, he found an unlatched conservatory window. He put in an arm and, after some groping, was able to open the adjacent door to the yard by turning the knob inside.

He passed through a darkened kitchen, where the utilitarian shapes of woodburning stove, heavy iron utensils, workbenches and a table and chairs loomed massively. In a hallway beyond was a series of doors, all closed except that to the consulting-room, which was empty.

Everywhere was the pervasive, unappealing fragrance of gardenia toilet-water mingled with carbolic. The McAdams smell.

A strip of light showed under one of the closed doors which by its position appeared to give on to a front parlour. Joshua glided stealthily to the door and eased it open.

The bearded doctor, wearing a nightshirt, was dozing in a rocking chair. An empty drinking glass stood on a side table close to his stubby-fingered hand.

Joshua took up a position looking down on him and declaimed with wrathful scorn, '. . . the innocent sleep, sleep that knits up the ravell'd sleave of care!'

McAdams came to with a start.

'D-Dillard! What in the Good Lord's name. . . ?'

'The Good Lord!' Joshua scoffed. 'Tell me, Doctor, doesn't your sanctimonious claptrap choke you? Or is it of a kind with Augusta Clamorgan's?'

'I d-don't know what you're talking about!' McAdams squeaked.

'I figure you do! Ramon Rubriz talked before he died. Confessed. It's your old pal John Clamorgan's widow who abducted Emily Greatheart, isn't it? She's eaten up with religious mania. A crazy woman! She aims to make the girl pay for the heinous crime of becoming engaged to be married to her darling son Frank.'

'Pardon me, but I don't—'

Joshua was brooking no flimsy excuses. 'Lies! You're a treacherous, slimy snake who's gone along with the foul business all along, because you want Augusta's hand in marriage, and to scoop up the Clamorgan fortune in land and stock.'

McAdams was taken aback by the informed extent of the accusations. He tried to force a note of outrage into his voice.

'You have it all wrong, sir! Mrs Clamorgan means Miss Greatheart no harm!' he blurted. 'I'll tell you how it is . . . just let me have some more brandy. It's been a long and harrowing night.'

Joshua grunted in the back of his throat. 'And it ain't over yet!'

He wasn't going to buy McAdams's protestations of his and Augusta Clamorgan's innocence in the horrific treatment meted out to Emily Greatheart by

Rubriz. But he made no move to stop McAdams as he took up his empty glass and tottered from the rocker to a sideboard.

'Mrs Clamorgan aims to convert Miss Greatheart – to reform her of her bad city habits and loose behaviour – so she'll be fit to share with her good self the memory of her fine and handsome son.'

Joshua snorted in ridicule and contempt.

'A load of bullshit, and you know it, McAdams! Miss Greatheart was no strumpet of the streets. The undeniable and tragic fact is that your patient's mind is on the wane, her mental processes diminished. You're her physician – the one she consults. You've a lot to answer for, and I mean to see you rot in a penitentiary for the loco schemes you've humoured and connived at. There'll be no remarriage for Mrs Clamorgan. She'll be lucky if she escapes permanent lodgment in a madhouse cell. But first you have to tell me where I find Emily Greatheart – even if I have to beat it out of your miserable carcass with my sore fists!'

McAdams slopped liquor into his glass. In his eagerness to fill it, splashes spilled on to the polished top of the sideboard.

Since he'd observed on previous occasions that the medico was fairly finicky, this alone should have warned Joshua. But he was weary and his brain was filled with thoughts of the misery which this evil man had failed to end for Emily Greatheart by deliberate inaction. Most urgent was the necessity to make him reveal her place of captivity.

Let McAdams drink if that was what it took to

loosen his tongue. He could then be on his way to rescue her. . . .

McAdams closed his eyes as he put the full glass to his lips. 'Uuuugh!' he shuddered.

'No!' Joshua snarled.

He dived at McAdams and grabbed his wrist, but the glass was empty. McAdams had swallowed the contents in a single gulp.

He laughed. 'You're too late, Dillard! You might've ruined my plans, but I've cheated you of success at the last. That draught was sixty per cent laudanum. I'll be dead before anyone can make me talk!'

'You bastard! You dirty coward!'

Joshua was livid, but knew anything he said was futile other than as a release for his own huge anger.

McAdams smiled with dreamy, malicious amusement.

'Words can't hurt me. . . .' His words tailed off.

Then, little by little, the harsh lines fear had chiselled into his face in reaction to Joshua's ferocity smoothed out and vanished. He laughed throatily and lurched back to his chair. He seemed to be asleep before he slumped into it.

Creakingly, it was set to rocking. But Joshua didn't hear it. He was out the door and out the house, heading for the bay horse and the Slash C ranch. Exhausted though he was, this night of violence was – like he'd said to McAdams – not over yet. There must be no stopping. . . .

Emily Greatheart trembled on the edge of hysteria.

'You,' she said. 'You!' Her eyes filled with horror and she stepped back. 'Why have you come? What do you want?'

Only instinctively did she know this visit was out of the ordinary, since all hours, day and night, were of the same texture in a windowless place with no light except a feeble candle's.

She retreated backwards across her musty prison from the most frightening of the three people who maintained her captivity.

Mrs Augusta Clamorgan, once her prospective mother-in-law, was the embodiment of an evil more stark and foul than any she could have met in her wildest nightmares.

The answers to Emily's questions were prefaced with a shrill scream of mocking laughter.

'You've fallen from grace and I've come to hear your confession, slut! Then we shall do what has to be done to purge you, and ensure you lose forever the wicked appetite for carnal practices.'

Augusta was dressed in a long black robe and a crucifix hung at her shapeless bosom. Despite this and her talk of confession, Emily knew she was no more Catholic than she was or Frank had been. Augusta's religious fervour was a macabre parody of what might have once been practised long ago by the founders of the Slash C ranch and the builders of the old church she'd made into a shrine to her dead son.

You had to humour the mad, didn't you?

'Don't be silly, Mrs Clamorgan,' Emily said, but her voice was too weak and her position too desperately inferior to make it sound any kind of authoritative advice, much less an order to a gibbering woman clean out of her mind.

Moreover, it caused the vinegary expression on Augusta's white and haggard face to intensify.

'Don't take that tone with me, missy. You're a shameless wanton! You deluded my son with your smooth city manners, and now you have my *mayordomo* in your toils. You've – *sinned* with him like a common prostitute!'

'That's a gross distortion of the truth! Your fine Señor Rubriz raped me!'

The older woman drew herself erect. The angular sharpness of her features, the scragginess about her neck and the blackness of her robe made her look like a bird of prey – a vulture.

'I won't listen to you, temptress! My son would be alive today were it not for your indecent picture stirring animal passions in the sons of respectable families.'

Emily gasped at the monstrous accusation. 'It was a most chaste likeness caught by a prizewinning Denver photographer, a friend of my father, and a dean of the profession.'

'There! You're immodest, full of self-idolatry,' Augusta croaked.

Emily had backed as far as the earthen wall. With nowhere else to go to escape the hateful face thrusting itself toward her, she nerved herself for a retaliation she knew to be totally foolish. Impetuously, she swung an open hand, knowing the act would do nothing to alleviate her plight.

The slap connected crisply, stinging her palm and leaving a red imprint on Augusta's bony cheek.

'Get away from me, you horrible hag!' she said between her teeth.

But the next moment the raving woman was on her, hitting out herself.

The women struggled. Augusta, the grieving mother, was more like an avenging fury. She clawed at Emily's face, missed and grabbed a handful of long, reddish-gold hair. She pulled viciously.

Tears came to Emily's eyes. She grabbed at the scrawny wrist and kicked. She didn't have the protection of even slippers, since footwear, along with the rest of her outer clothes had long been taken from her. The kick hurt her bare toes, but gave her the satisfaction of a grunt from Augusta and the release of her hair.

The fight wasn't over. Augusta got her clawing hands on Emily's soft torso, taking cruel grips of whatever she could, seeking viciously to do damage. Emily was pinned, writhing, against the wall. She felt her already ripped camisole being torn from her scratched body once more.

Augusta's breath was coming in harsh pants; Emily's in frantic sobs. Soon, the older woman, driven by the strength of her madness, had the upper hand.

An arm coming free, Emily clenched her fist and swung a punch. Augusta twisted away from it, and at the same time placed an arm-jolting blow of her own on Emily's chin.

Though no knockout punch, Emily had spent

weeks cooped up in semi-dark, near-airless captivity, climaxed by Ramon Rubriz's exhausting abuse. They had taken a toll. Augusta's punch jerked her head back into the wall. The double thud made her weak head ring and she slipped to the dirt floor, only just conscious.

Augusta bent and grabbed her ankles. She pulled her till she was in middle of the room, before throwing down her legs wide, so she was spreadeagled and barely covered by the tatters of her scanty garments.

'Please – please!' Emily sobbed. 'I'll get my father to send you money. Only leave me alone, just don't touch me. I've been hurt enough. Oh, please!'

It was then, from a pocket in the folds of her black robe that Augusta produced a metallic object. In the semi-darkness, a gleam of candlelight shone on it, showing its clean, surgical sharpness.

Terrified, Emily saw it was a skinning knife.

'I've only just begun with you, trollop! For the cleansing of your soul, your body must give up its most sinful part . . . so you'll be pure when you rejoin my Frank as his bride in Heaven.'

Augusta's mental instability made her a frightening figure. The pressure upon her rocking mind of what she'd heard of Ramon Rubriz's conduct was more than she could cope with. Her dubious sanity had snapped, allowing her to paint Emily completely as a loose, alien woman who'd betrayed her son's memory, maybe her son himself. She'd convinced herself she had a role and a duty in Emily's expiation.

Emily could conceive of no worse purgatory than what she would endure at the hands of a madwoman with a knife.

The veins bulged from Augusta's forehead; frenzy was consuming her like fire. She stepped between Emily's legs and knelt, glittering blade in hand.

14

HOUSE OF
THE DEAD

Joshua Dillard ran back to where he'd left the bay
horse. The animal was growing accustomed to his
wild ways, seemed to know what the erratic *norteamer-*
icano expected from a mount. She was ready to
respond to the murmur of his firm voice, the pressure of his knees and heels, the strong pull of his
hand on the reins. When he tightened the cinch and
swung into the saddle, she leaped off into the darkness at a game gallop.

Joshua flicked the rein ends. 'Go, gal, go!'

Clearing town and setting the horse's nose for the
Slash C, Joshua urged her into a raking, reckless
pace. Hoofs drummed a fierce tattoo.

His thoughts were bleak. 'God! What can be
happening in that place? Just to get there in
time. . . .'

Nor did he spare himself. By sheer willpower, he took an iron grip on his flagging body, forcing himself to stay upright in the uncomfortable Mexican saddle with disregard for the physical agonies that racked him. He wasn't played out yet. . . .

A bright, near-full moon hung high, playing hide-and-seek with the low, drifting clouds. And Joshua was an accomplished horseman who'd ridden many a time in darkness, rain or mist on the most urgent of missions.

The mare was undaunted by the late ride, totally familiar with every rise and dip of the valley grassland, every subtle twist and turn of the trail back to the home stable. Joshua gave her her head, intuitively putting his trust in her knowledge, even when cloud shadows darkened the way ahead.

The cool of the passing air as he rushed through the night did little to cool the fire in Joshua's brain. Since he'd arrived in the Welcome Valley country, action in the investigation had come thick and fast. But steps had been made backward as well as forward. He still didn't know where Emily Greatheart was, any more than he had when he'd arrived in Pike's Crossing to be challenged instantly by the aggressively defensive Wallers and duped by Denholm McAdams.

When he'd seen McAdams take poison, he'd felt a sudden hot rage and an almost uncontrollable urge to stomp the dying man to an unrecognizable pulp. With him went the best available answers to key questions and the fastest way to rescuing Emily, if she was alive.

The Wallers, of course, had been a red-herring from the start. He'd been too clever by three-fourths in wasting his time and energy in incurring their wrath.

The lucky break had been spotting Ramon Rubriz's bay horse and being able to identify the animal as the bushwhacker's. But Rubriz, as much as McAdams and Vince Waller, had killed himself. So it could be the bay horse was the best and only ally he'd made.

He rode the mare hell-for-leather. At the end of his journey awaited more questions to be asked of people with twisted minds. Both of them, he reflected morosely, were women. Beating answers out of them was therefore out of the question, but only with their answers might the daughter of Big Jack Greatheart be saved.

The bay made swift time to the Slash C. He thundered along the straight trail to the silent cluster of ranch buildings and flung himself from the lathered, exhausted horse outside the *hacienda*. The big, white-washed house beyond the mariposa tree was bathed in a pure and silvery light, but Joshua could think only of the corruption that festered under its blemish-free surface.

The yard gate was already open and he stormed through to hammer on the heavy oaken door with such force that the brittle wreath to Frank Clamorgan was dislodged and fell in a dusty heap to the porch steps.

In response to his thunderous knock, he heard hurried footsteps on the tiled floor within and mutterings of complaint. He recognized the voice as Francisca Rubriz's.

'*Madre de Dios!*' she cried as she opened the door, which had been closed but not bolted. 'Would you wake the dead, *señor?*'

The rhetorical question was one Joshua would have been hard put to answer. Plainly word had yet to reach the Slash C of the night's incidents in Pike's Crossing. The woman didn't know he'd been obliged to shoot dead her rotten husband . . . that she was a widow.

But it occurred to him she'd not been summoned from sleep. Insufficient time had elapsed from when he'd begun his knocking. Also, she was dressed, was carrying a small, lighted lantern, and was in a wakeful, disgruntled mood which went beyond sudden annoyance at his peremptory assault on the door.

'*Señora*, there must be no argument about this,' Joshua said. 'I'm seeing Mrs Clamorgan without delay.'

He brushed past her into the long whitewashed corridor bisecting the *hacienda*. Which door would lead him to Augusta Clamorgan and her secrets?

'What are you doing!' she exclaimed.

'Where do I find her?' he rapped.

'You are rude, *amigo mio!*' Francisca tossed back. 'Not in the house, I will tell you that.'

'Ah, then she's gone to her chapel and her prisoner, is that it?'

Francisca's face drained of colour and her eyes widened at mention of the word prisoner.

Joshua knew he'd scored at least a partial hit.

144

Exultant, he amplified his question.

'Come, Señora Rubriz, denial is useless now. Miss Emily Greatheart is held captive here, isn't she?'

The woman glared at him sullenly, refusing to give him yea or nay. 'I can say nothing.'

'So you're in on this, too, are you?' Joshua said distastefully. 'There's no pride to be had in what you're doing. I think it's time you reconsidered your position.'

'I can say nothing,' she repeated.

Joshua suspected Francisca had been raised in neighbouring New Mexico Territory, if not Mexico itself, probably in an environment where the things that mattered were the faith, a husband, the ranch, unswerving loyalty to *el patrón* and his family. The Slash C retained features of a ranch model still prevalent in New Mexico.

He tried a different tack. 'Take me to Miss Greatheart!'

'I will do nothing.'

'Damn you! Let me tell you this – when I do find her, and the truth's spilled, it won't go well for you! What Augusta Clamorgan pays you isn't worth going to the gallows for.'

He wheeled from her sulky, belligerent face and strode from the house.

Fatigue was grinding him down, but relentlessly he headed for the old church.

Emily Greatheart fought the fear that utterly paralysed her. She couldn't move, could only lie vulnerably and stare as Augusta Clamorgan came at her with the glinting skinning knife.

Even when the mad woman stooped over her and clawed up her petticoat still higher, she couldn't move, couldn't shout. Augusta poised the knife, mouthing obscenity in an incongruous tone of righteous smugness. She was plumb loco, full of gleeful elation at the mutilation she about to accomplish.

Then, as the knife began to fall to make its hateful incision, life pumped back into Emily.

She twisted frantically, reaching up and knocking the knife aside. Red-hot pain seared the back of her hand as the razor-sharp blade cut the skin over her knuckles.

Augusta Clamorgan lost her grip on the knife, which spun loose to thud point-first into the earthen floor. With a cry of rage, she sprang on to Emily, sitting astride her and pinning her between her bony knees. In her weakened state, Emily found her incredibly strong, even heavy.

'Still the wildcat, eh?' Augusta croaked. 'But squeamish about the knife. Well, we can have no more fancy excuses. Fine lady you were! You behaved with Ramon worse than a whore in a sequined dress! The deed has got to be done before you can be despatched to my darling Frank. . . .'

She reached out to retrieve the knife.

The terror of hurt, of pain, was as strong as ever, but Emily didn't know whether she had it in her to continue to fight. She felt her time in a nightmare world was running out fast.

Joshua dashed into what he thought of as the desecrated church to find it empty. Nothing stirred except the flickering flames of fourteen long, twisted candles that illuminated the idolatrous portrait of Frank Clamorgan occupying the place of honour high on the railed altar.

Panic gripped him, racing his heart, fraying his nerves. Had Francisca lied when she'd said Augusta Clamorgan wasn't in the house? Where was the blasted woman? Had he come this far to be fooled with?

His client's daughter had been ruthlessly attacked according to her attacker's own mockery of a last confession of his sins. At this moment, she might be lying somewhere close, dying.

He raked the shadows with sore eyes, searching for the clues that had to be somewhere. Suddenly, he noticed a place where the dusty red tapestry was bunched, and was sure it hadn't been that way when he'd been in the place the day prior.

His hopes jumped as he recalled, too, the mysterious noises he couldn't locate and which Doctor McAdams had explained were made by pigeons in a bell tower. Was there a door there to another chamber?

He took a half-dozen quick steps and dragged the tapestry aside. It did act as a curtain to an arched door!

A wild cry of triumph welled out of his throat. Without hesitation he threw himself at the door, bursting its flimsy lock.

His momentum almost plunged him headlong down a steep flight of stone steps, but he was able to retain a teetering balance by thrusting the palms of his much-abused hands against the rough-cast walls.

He called out, 'Is there anyone down there?'

No reply ... except an echo; a charnel-house smell when he replenished his breath.

He returned briefly to the nave to vault the rail around the altar and to purloin one of the tall, lighted candles, wrenching it from a gilt holder. Trailing coils of oily black smoke, he took it with him to descend the stairs.

They gave access to a small crypt, gloomy and dank and totally dominated by a stone sarcophagus of new construction.

The masons had done a beautiful job crafting the resting place for the remains of Frank, beloved son of the late John and Augusta Clamorgan of Welcome Valley, Arizona. But Joshua Dillard was out of luck again. The depressing place was otherwise empty.

No stricken Emily. No Mrs Clamorgan devotedly whispering prayers to a God who was probably her lost boy himself.

15

THE LAST SHOTS

Joshua conducted a swift search of the church, his
frustration mounting. In despair, he concluded
Augusta Clamorgan's private chapel had no other
secrets. It contained no cell below; no hiding-place in
the bell tower reached by rickety ladders – though
birds of some sort did squawk at his brief intrusion by
night into their domain.

His face stony and bleak, Joshua left the church.
The cold in the place had been of a high and different order, but nonetheless he shivered as he
returned to the night air and cast his eyes over he
clustered, mostly log-and-adobe ranch buildings,
from the ugly, isolated cube of the powderhouse to
jacals, to the handsome *hacienda* with its red-tiled
roof that looked black in the moonlight.

Far off, coyotes yapped and owls hooted dismally.
Once a cougar screeched from a far ridge, its chilling
cry echoing across the valley to be flung back by the

foothills of the broken country – a taunting reminder of his wild-goose chase to the abandoned Spanish mine, where Emily hadn't been, but Bart Waller's men had, waiting to exact retribution for their initial humiliating defeat at Pike's Crossing's Grand Hotel.

It had all taken place in less than two days, but to Joshua, seasoned fighter though he was, it seemed a lifetime of strain and pain. Almost asleep on his feet he might be, but he couldn't give up yet.

He stomped back to the house where Francisca Rubriz met him with grinning contempt and unsmiling dark eyes.

'Big, clever *hombre*, but you find nothing! It will be finished very soon now and you cannot stop it. Leave, pighead!'

Certain Francisca Rubriz knew where he could find Emily Greatheart and the crazed woman who was holding her, Joshua again debated with himself whether he could beat the truth out of her. But she was, at end of all, a woman. He couldn't do it.

Yet he could use words, and maybe they would be as brutal and effective as fists: surely Francisca Rubriz's opposition would be broken by the stark news her unfaithful husband was dead!

'No, I'll not leave without Emily Greatheart,' he said sternly. 'Now hear this – your husband was killed tonight in a gunfight in town. With his dying breath, he bragged how he'd cheated on you by taking his pleasure with Augusta Clamorgan's tempting prisoner. Señora Clamorgan's mad schemes are at the root this grief. You owe her nothing – not a plugged centavo – for the great injury she has done you.'

Francisca was dumbfounded. Her dark eyes became pinpoints and her lips quivered. 'I do not believe you!' she said jerkily.

Joshua shrugged callously. 'Just the truth, Señora Rubriz, just the truth. I witnessed it myself before I rode here to rescue Señorita Greatheart.'

A savage snarl formed around the Mexican woman's clenched teeth. 'I will kill the bitch!' she hissed. 'Both the bitches!'

Her venom was passionate and frightening, but before Joshua could press her more, she darted back into the *hacienda* and, despite the whitewashed walls, was lost to him in the lampless gloom.

Joshua went after her. He heard a door slam, and struck a match that showed him many doors, all as equally shut and blank. He heard a thud and flung wide the one from behind which he thought it must have come. It opened into a bedroom, full of heavy, dark furniture. A drawer in a dresser had been pulled out and dropped to the floor, its contents – including what at a glance looked like rags and a small can of oil – spilled. Another door, glazed, gave on to a paved patio. Its flimsy curtain fluttered in the breeze.

Joshua went across the bedroom in a bound, and was rewarded with the sight of Francisca turning a corner from the enclosed patio into the outer walled yard.

He was on her trail. Soon he would be on her heels.

But as Joshua left the house's enclosure, the fleeing woman turned. In her hand, as if by magic, there appeared a revolver.

It was a big, hefty piece of armament, with a barrel about nine inches long. Joshua's expert eye placed it, possibly, as an old Walker Colt which in total length would measure more than fifteen inches. Not exactly a lady's pistol, Joshua thought, and forged on relentlessly.

'Stop!' he ordered. 'That ancient piece of hardware will be useless to you.'

But Francisca, to his surprise, was not a complete greenhorn in her handling of the fearsome weapon. She lifted it, clenching the one-piece walnut grips in both hands exactly as Joshua himself would have advised had it been essential she should attempt to fire it. Her feet were firmly planted, two feet apart.

Then she squeezed the trigger in the approved manner. The massive gun roared and bucked in her hands.

The 220-grain conical bullet whizzed over Joshua's head and slammed into the outer wall of the house's yard. Pieces of adobe and fine dust flew everywhere. But Joshua had dropped flat to the ground. Only one shot fired so far, but the old repeating pistol, a specimen of the model that had gotten Sam Colt back on his feet after a spell of bankruptcy in the 1840s, still held another five in its six .44 calibre cylinders. Facts like these Joshua respected.

By the time he'd cautiously raised his head, Francisca was off running again. She'd gone past the largely empty corrals and was heading in a westerly direction, slightly uphill and away from the Slash C settlement.

Joshua frowned. Nothing lay in that direction, no dwellings, no barns or stables. Nothing except the disused powderhouse! Ugly, set well apart . . . a thick-walled, stone-and-adobe rectangle with no windows.

'*That's the powderhouse where explosives were stored for use in the mine,*' Denholm McAdams had said. '*Young Frank was going to put it to use again when his mine machinery arrived from Denver.*'

All at once, the final pieces fell into place and Joshua knew where Emily Greatheart had been hidden for so many weeks from all eyes and ears.

Joshua knew it was time for him to take his chances. He sprinted after Francisca and the gamble didn't cost him his life. The woman didn't turn and fire again but kept going, strong legs pumping with a determination of her own. Which was as well, since a Walker Colt was known to be as effective as a common rifle at one hundred yards, and superior to a musket even at two hundred.

Joshua gained on the woman rapidly. She was breathless as well as distraught by the time their thudding feet brought them close to the squat, featureless building. The place, Joshua saw, had an iron door, like a bank vault's. A big brass padlock, open and with a key jutting from it, hung from the hasp.

And the door was outlined by the thinnest line of light at one side where it was ajar. Plainly, no one in their right mind would take a burning candle or lantern into the repository . . . if it was being used for its designed purpose – the safekeeping of blasting powder.

Everything confirmed this was the place where Emily was confined.

And Francisca was scant yards from the door, toting a gun like a hand cannon and which she'd shown she was capable of using. Maybe Joshua's tactics had been too successful. Learning of her husband's death had made Francisca reveal what he wanted to know, sure. But the Mexican was a woman of hot-blooded temperament and he'd also sparked in her an overpowering desire for vengeance. Her intent was murder!

It was clear to Joshua she'd convinced herself Emily Greatheart was the author of her misfortunes. Jealous from the start, she thought the worst of the stranger from Denver and was determined to blame her rather than her husband – or even herself – for his infidelity. The career in rustling that in fact had led to his death counted for nothing.

Gone cold, Joshua plucked the Peacemaker from his holster and cocked it. At fifty yards, it would be a longish shot, and even the Peacemaker's long barrel wouldn't guarantee a man on the move accuracy.

Suddenly, all bets on his marksmanship were off.

The massive outer door to the powderhouse swung wide and two women rushed out into the moonlight. It was an astonishing spectacle. The first was a young person with a bloody hand and in tattered, filthy underclothing, pale-faced and hugely anguished. The second was Augusta Clamorgan, wielding a knife.

'Bawd! Hussy!' Augusta screamed. 'You sent my son to the hereafter! You must atone before you can stand before him and God!'

Her black gown filled with the breeze and billowed out behind her like the wings of a bird of prey.

Emily, for it could be no other, sobbed and ran.

With all three women all moving and in close proximity to each other, Joshua knew any shooting was out of the question, let alone a trick, disarming shot.

But Francisca, whose desire was for blood and death, had no such compunctions. She gave a high-pitched laugh.

'Heaven and your pretty son be damned, *señora*! I'll send the city whore to hell!'

She swung up and shakily aimed the Walker Colt's solid four pounds, nine ounces of iron and brass. Again she took a double-handed hold. There was a flash and a roar.

Her novice shot went past Emily and smashed into the flat chest of Augusta Clamorgan, who was thrown to the ground, possibly never knowing what hit her, her front neatly holed, fatally damaged internally. Simultaneously, the knife flew high from her outflung hand, sparkling wickedly in the silver light before burying itself point first in the ground.

With a howl of rage, Francisca then once more turned the gun on Emily, avid for her revenge on the girl.

Joshua was on to her in a final bound. He grabbed the smoking gun and tore it from her unresisting grip.

'For God's sake – enough!' he said. 'It's over.'

Unnoticed, a pale lemon fringe of light was etching the far eastern rim of the valley.

Over it was: a mercy mission that had begun and ended in a maelstrom of violence. Two days later, Joshua and Emily were riding the rails north to Denver. He was escorting her home, well pleased with the successful outcome of his investigation.

Big Jack Greatheart had been telegraphed the good news of his daughter's safety and was understood to be immensely relieved and happy. Joshua, having had to spend what was left of his expenses money on new clothes in Pike's Crossing, was looking forward to collecting his fee in Denver. For once, he wasn't looking like a saddle tramp and soon he would be entirely out of the red.

'How much further is it?' Emily asked from her corner window seat in the railroad car.

The clackety-clack of the narrow-gauge rails under the wheels, the jounce and sway of the speeding car, were gradually lulling Joshua off to more of the sleep he still needed to catch up on. But he was content to answer his weary but recovering companion.

'That was Pueblo we last passed through. So we've about another hundred miles to cover to Denver. Mind, that shouldn't try our patience – we've already done two hundred from Santa Fe.'

The trip was reputed to be one of scenic grandeur. It was this, as well as economic value, that had inspired General William Jackson Palmer to build his railroad to the south, but since it was coming full dark, the scenery was largely invisible to the two travellers. A conductor came through the car, lighting the kerosene lamps. Then all Joshua and Emily could see was their own reflections in window glass gone shiny black.

Emily sighed and settled back in her seat.

'I thank God for the miracle that you found me, and just in time to stop either of those angry women killing me. I'm afraid I made a poor and rash choice for a husband in Frank Clamorgan, and paid a high price.'

'Well, I hope it's the last price you pay,' Joshua said. 'Finding you was indeed fortuitous at the last – like a big game of thimblerig.'

'How was that?'

'Thimblerig is the old shell game. The dealer hides a pea under one of three shells. The gambler takes his pick of the shells. I turned over two shells – Frank's abandoned Spanish mine and his mother's old church. But all the time you were under the third, which was the powderhouse with its two-foot-thick walls.'

'How aptly put, Mr Dillard!'

Joshua laughed off her praise. 'The analogy is scarcely the product of my own imagination. Would that I'd had more! No, in some places I do believe they play a variation of the thimble game with cards, using the Queen as the pea. They call it "Hunt the Lady".'

The pleasantries and the laughter were among the last they were to share. For when they finally reached Big Jack Greatheart's home in Denver, they were met on the doorstep by the nurse and housekeeper, Mrs Fardell. She was both distressed and pleased to see them.

It appeared Joshua's hope was misplaced and Emily had one more price to pay for her unfortunate association with the spoiled son of an Arizonan cattle family.

Tearfully, Mrs Fardell explained.

'Your dad had been mighty lonesome for you, Miss Greatheart, and he was that plumb happy when he heard you were safe, he took a turn and died at dawn. Heart failure, the doctors said. But he went as he lived – with a brave spirit. He'd gotten real frail with the fretting. It ate up what was left of him by the arthritis. I'd say he was sick unto death. How he held out so long was a marvel to me that nursed him. The end was merciful.'

To Emily, a chip off the old block, and who'd lately gone through so many perils, it was another sadness she would overcome.

Joshua stayed in Denver for the funeral of the veteran frontier lawman and to see that Emily was safely re-established with a few old friends.

When Emily tried to press upon him the fee agreed with her father for her return to Denver, he stoutly refused it.

Joshua knew the hypocritical morality of his day. Men were allowed to live by double standards, but 'good' women were ruled by the sacred Single Standard, from which there couldn't be even the unjust suggestion of a lapse. After the shocking and sensational episode in Arizona, Emily had a lot in her life to forget and to be forgotten. Her story was an outrage to prim minds. They would welcome no reminder of it in their polite company. It might upset their social conscience.

One day, Joshua was sure, Emily would meet a steady young man who'd be willing to marry her, because she'd survived still vivacious and handsome, plus courageously strong-minded like her father. A delightful personality she'd lost during her extremity was re-emerging. But her chances had been seriously prejudiced, and meantime she'd need every dollar to support herself so she could live as a decent girl should.

Joshua said, 'You've lost too much already. I can't leave you without money as well as without family. If you were inheriting a million, I wouldn't take a bent cent from you. It wouldn't be right.'

Shortly after, he moved on from Denver seeking new employment for his singular talents that met his preferences.

And he went, as he invariably did, empty-pocketed.